HARLEQUIN®
Presents

What have we got for you in Harlequin Presents books this month? Some of the most gorgeous men you're ever likely to meet!

With *His Royal Love-Child*, Lucy Monroe brings you another installment in her gripping and emotional trilogy, ROYAL BRIDES; Prince Marcello Scorsolini has a problem—his mistress is pregnant! Meanwhile, in Jane Porter's sultry, sexy new story, *The Sheikh's Disobedient Bride*, Tally is being held captive in Sheikh Tair's harem...because he intends to tame her! If it's a Mediterranean tycoon that you're hoping for, Jacqueline Baird has just the guy for you in *The Italian's Blackmailed Mistress*: Max Quintano, ruthless in his pursuit of Sophie, whom he's determined to bed using every means at his disposal! In Sara Craven's *Wife Against Her Will*, Darcy Langton is stunned when she finds herself engaged to businessman Joel Castille—traded as part of a business merger! The glamour continues with *For Revenge...Or Pleasure?*—the latest title in our popular miniseries FOR LOVE OR MONEY, written by Trish Morey, truly is romance on the red carpet! If it's a classic read you're after, try *His Secretary Mistress* by Chantelle Shaw. She pens her first sensual and heartwarming story for the Presents line with a tall, dark and handsome British hero, whose feisty yet vulnerable secretary tries to keep a secret about her private life that he won't appreciate.

Check out www.eHarlequin.com for a list of recent Presents books! Enjoy!

Introducing a brand-new miniseries

This is romance on the red carpet!

FOR LOVE OR MONEY is the ultimate
reading experience for the reader who loves
Harlequin Presents® books, and who also has a
taste for tales of wealth and celebrity—
and the accompanying gossip and scandal!

Available only from Harlequin Presents®

Trish Morey

FOR REVENGE...OR PLEASURE?

For *Love* OR MONEY

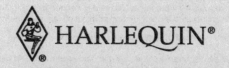

HARLEQUIN®

TORONTO • NEW YORK • LONDON
AMSTERDAM • PARIS • SYDNEY • HAMBURG
STOCKHOLM • ATHENS • TOKYO • MILAN • MADRID
PRAGUE • WARSAW • BUDAPEST • AUCKLAND

ISBN 0-373-12545-3

FOR REVENGE...OR PLEASURE?

First North American Publication 2006.

All about the author...
Trish Morey

TRISH MOREY wrote her first book at age eleven for a children's book-week competition; entitled *Island Dreamer,* it proved to be her first rejection. Shattered and broken, she turned to a life where she could combine her love of fiction with her need for creativity—and became a chartered accountant. ☺ Life wasn't all dull though, as she embarked on a skydiving course, completing three jumps before deciding that she'd given her fear of heights a run for its money.

Meanwhile, she fell in love and married a handsome guy who cut computer code. After the birth of their second daughter, Trish spied an article saying that Harlequin was actively seeking new authors. It was one of those eureka moments—Trish was going to be one of those authors!

Eleven years after reading that fateful article, the magical phone call came and Trish finally realized her dream. According to Trish, writing and selling a book is a major life achievement that ranks right up there with jumping out of an airplane and motherhood. All three take commitment, determination and sheer guts, but the effort is so very, very worthwhile.

Trish now lives with her husband and four young daughters in a special part of south Australia, surrounded by orchards and bushland and visited by the occasional koala and kangaroo.

You can visit Trish at her Web site at www.trishmorey.com or e-mail her at trish@trishmorey.com.

For my editors, past and present.

To Angelina Manzano, my first ever editor,
who made the magical call that turned my
long-held dreams into reality.

And to Emma Dunford, whose eternal patience
and unstinting encouragement are this
painfully slow writer's best friends.

Thank you both!

CHAPTER ONE

SO THIS was the A-List? From his vantage point on the less crowded mezzanine, Loukas Demakis narrowed his eyes and scanned the sea of glittering celebrities milling about below in the Beverly Hills mansion's ballroom. He suppressed a sneer as his gaze slid over the megastars, the wannabes and the otherwise rich and famous, all trying to out-dazzle each other with their designer clothes, designer bodies, and enough bling-bling to light up Times Square.

And all of it so fake!

His jaw clenched, teeth grinding together. This wasn't his world. The sooner he was out of here the better.

But first he had a job to do. The words of his father rang loud in his memory—'Get her away from them. I don't care what it takes or who gets hurt—just get her out of there!'

And, dammit, after what had happened to Zoë, there was no way he would let his sister so much as be touched by any of them. He'd do whatever it took to stop her. He'd do whatever it took to keep her safe!

The crowd swayed apart as a woman strode up to the dais. *Two women.* He pressed closer to the balustrade, his fingers tightening around the rail.

It had to be them. The sorcerer and her apprentice.

Cheers and applause erupted from the crowd when his instincts proved right and Dr Grace Della-Bosca was introduced. A woman in a golden gown stepped up to the microphone. He peered closer. For someone he knew to be on the wrong side of fifty she was remarkably well-preserved. Tutankhamen's bride wearing Dolce & Gabbana. But then, eternal youth was her business.

He'd meant to listen to what she had to say. He started to listen. Until the second woman turned towards the crowd and smiled, and the breath ripped out of him as if he'd taken a blow to the body.

Jade Ferraro.

This was the woman he'd come to meet. This was the woman he'd come to question. In the flesh.

And what flesh!

Where Della-Bosca's skin looked as if it had been stretched to within an inch of its life, the younger woman's was smooth and flawless, her features arranged on her face in a way that found the idea of classic good looks wanting. Clear almond-shaped blue eyes echoed a smile that was wide—almost too wide—though her lips looked lush enough to take the width and then some.

But her face was only one part of the package. Her honey-coloured hair was swept into a sleek coil that exposed the long sweep of her neck to her surprisingly modest neckline.

And the dress! There was nothing modest about it—it must have been shrink-wrapped around her. Without the shimmering aqua colour of the material it would have been impossible to tell where her skin ended and the fabric began, the way it hugged tight over her breasts, dipping into the curves and skimming over the flat of her stomach. The gown was a total failure in terms of disguising the shape beneath, and yet there was no doubt peeling it off would still be an exercise in discovery. An exercise for which he'd be only too happy to volunteer.

With a growl laced with acerbity he clamped down on the traitorous response of his body.

Of course she was a looker. She was bound to be! Because there was no doubt her attributes owed more to the skilled hands of Dr Grace Della-Bosca, the mother superior of the high church of cosmetic surgery, than to any generous endowment by Mother Nature. She was a walking advertisement for the witch doctor's talents.

The speech came to an end and the crowd once again broke into applause. The younger woman turned back towards the dais a fraction, and then hesitated, her hands locked together as if frozen mid-clap. Then her head swivelled back over her shoulder, her chin lifted and swept up across the crowd, until her eyes jagged and stuck rock-solid on his.

He saw them widen in shocked perplexity; he saw the fractional coming together of her brows as she battled for recognition. He even fancied he felt the tremors spreading out from the quake that rippled through her, and in that instant he decided on a new and much more satisfying course of attack. He allowed himself a smile as his body hummed its approval of his plan.

It hadn't been his choice to come here tonight, but just because he had to mix with a crowd of people he had nothing in common with and even less respect for it didn't mean he couldn't enjoy the mission he was on. Why should he settle for just questions and answers when he could have so much more? Why shouldn't he find out what Jade Ferraro was really made of?

'Run all you like, Jade Ferraro,' he muttered as she spun away and disappeared into the throng of people surrounding the famous cosmetic surgeon. 'But I will have you.'

Someone pressed a glass of champagne into her hand and her first impulse was to hold the moistly beaded flute to her head to cool her heated brow. She wasn't sure what had happened just then, but the experience of meeting that intense dark gaze had left her almost reeling.

Then the orchestra started playing, and couples were swirling around, and suddenly it was too hot, too loud, and much too claustrophobic in the crowded ballroom.

She heard her name and snapped her attention away from the glass. 'So, tell me how you think it went,' Grace insisted, sounding impatient, as if it wasn't the first time she'd framed the question.

'Oh, absolutely wonderful,' Jade assured her, kissing her mentor on each cheek, knowing the woman she admired more than anyone in the world would have been just that—despite the fact she couldn't re-call a thing beyond Grace's thanks to everyone for attending the fundraiser. But then, it was impossible to remember anything aside from the prickly sensation that someone had been watching her, and the blast-furnace heat that had confronted her eyes once she'd found the source.

She took a deep breath, trying to dispel the lingering echoes of the strange sensation, trying to ignore the questions that remained unresolved in her mind. Who was that man? Why had he been watching her?

But someone else's eyes were on her now, someone else was waiting for a response, and questions about the owner of one powerfully intense pair of eyes that had seemed able to pierce right through to her soul had to be shoved aside. Because tonight was all about the world-famous Dr Della-Bosca, and the foundation established in her name. Nothing should be allowed to distract her from that.

This time the smile she allowed herself was heart-felt.

'The evening is a runaway success,' Jade assured the older woman. 'And you're the star,' she continued with more enthusiasm. 'Funds from tonight will set up your Saving Faces Foundation for years.'

'Yes,' Grace finally acknowledged, with a smile echoed in one expertly shaped eyebrow as she cast her eyes around the celebrity-filled ballroom. 'We must have done well.'

'It's a total credit to you, Grace,' a gruff male voice cut in. 'Our city could do with more corporate citizens like you.'

'Mayor Goldfinch,' Grace said with obvious delight as she was swept up into the distinguished-looking gentleman's embrace. 'And I thought our favourite foundation trustee wasn't able to make it tonight.'

'Knowing this night meant so much to you, how could I stay away? I pulled some strings and here I am.'

Jade allowed herself a smile as she made a tactical

withdrawal, certain that neither would notice anyway. The widower Mayor had made no secret of the fact he was looking for a new wife, and with a fortune made from his property development business there was no shortage of candidates. But it was Grace who was most frequently pictured on his arm, and it was clear that whatever feelings he had for Grace were reciprocated.

And Grace worked so hard, Jade reflected, switching her champagne for a glass of mineral water from the tray of a passing waiter; she so deserved to find a partner. She deserved to be happy.

A swirl of red fabric across the room and a flash of firm cleavage caught her eye. Rachael Delaney, her mind registered instantly. Twenty-year-old Southern belle and regular client of the Della-Bosca Clinic, who'd spent the last two years taking the TV soap world by storm and was now making a play for fame and fortune in the big league. And, from the way her recently enhanced breasts were spilling out of the slashed-to-the-navel line of her gown in the direction of the producer she was courting, it was clear Rachael was hoping the results of her latest procedure might just get her the movie contract she hungered for to-night.

Good luck to her, Jade thought, as she sipped on her mineral water, given she'd invested so much money in making herself look good—from the curve of her plumped lips to the sparkle in her skilfully upturned eyes. Jade could tick off the changes the Della-Bosca Clinic had made like checking off inventory.

'Not in the mood for celebrating?'

She didn't have to turn. The heated rush of sensation that rolled down her spine and unfurled into her extremities was all the confirmation she needed. That deep voice had to be the perfect accompaniment to the pair of piercing dark eyes that had left their imprint stamped all too deeply on her senses.

And somehow she knew it was important not to give in to her desire to turn straight away. Somehow she knew she had to continue to focus on something, anything, if she was going to maintain a hold on reality—her reality.

'What's it to you?' she responded, keeping her voice surprisingly light even as her back stiffened against his prickling proximity. She didn't know who he was, but she was in no hurry to be pinned under that potent stare again.

Instead she kept her gaze locked on Rachael as if she was holding onto a lifeline. Rachael was her link to reality, her excuse not to turn, and her instinctive defence against this strange out-of-her-depth feeling that seemed to go hand in hand with this stranger's presence.

But suddenly something blocked her view.

Not something.

Someone.

Him!

She sucked in a breath as broad shoulders filled her vision. And once again the man who'd been looking down from the mezzanine stared at her—except this time his piercing eyes were barely inches away. And, just as before, she felt the heat blasting from their penetrating brown depths in a confusing mixture of danger combined with a heart-stopping magnetism.

'Have we met?' she asked, kicking up her chin and knowing full well that she'd never seen the man before—in or out of the clinic. Having put the invitation list together, she knew he wasn't on it. Which meant he had to be someone's partner...

Lucky them.

The thought was so unwelcome she tried to quash it outright, but there was no chance of that—not when it was so true. Every part of this man seemed a perfect part of the whole—his slick dark hair, his chiselled bone structure, lips that were not too thin, not too full, and a body that promised to be every bit as well put together.

His lips turned into the barest smile. 'Maybe it's time we did.'

She waited for him to introduce himself, but he offered not a scrap of information more, failing to reveal who he was or why he was there, and impatience clicked logic back into gear, snapping her out of her frozen stance.

'I'm sorry, Mr Whoever-you-are, but I have invited guests to look after. I really don't have time to play games.'

She made to move away, but his velvet words stopped her in her tracks.

'And if you had the time?'

She stopped and blinked, forcing her back ramrod-straight in defence. She looked over her shoulder at him. 'Excuse me?'

'If you had the time, would you be more inclined to play?'

Warm shivers assaulted her flesh. Was it the effect of his rich deep voice, or was it because she almost hoped he just might mean it? Something about the man was compelling. Damn, *everything* about the man was compelling. And something about her own body's reaction impelled her to believe him.

'I don't play games.' She arched an eyebrow in his direction for effect.

'Pity,' he said. 'Such a waste.'

'Not really,' she replied, raising her chin with the certainty that she was about to have the final word. 'Because when I play, I play for keeps.'

She turned away, allowing herself a smile, feeling she'd won some kind of moral victory at least. Besides, the encounter had left her tingling with excitement. He might have thrown her completely at the start, but she'd enjoyed the attention from someone who appeared way more three-dimensional than the usual Beverly Hills society, with their egocentric conversation and their rapid-fire evaluation of who you were and how you might be of any use to them.

But she hadn't taken more than two steps before his rich laughter snagged into her consciousness, drawing her around as easily as a gentle finger press.

Except the way he looked at her and the set of his large, strong body, like the king of the jungle about to pounce and devour its prey, wiped out her feeling of superiority in an instant.

'In that case,' he said, his dark eyes crinkling at the sides, yet still filled with intensity that took her breath away, 'let the games begin.'

CHAPTER TWO

HE'D eliminated the distance between them, had reached out and taken hold of her hand before she could react. She gasped at his warmth, at the sculpted perfection of his hand and at his gentle touch, while fully aware of the latent strength lurking beneath.

Without taking his eyes from hers he carried her hand to his mouth. She'd expected just a brief kiss, and was vaguely aware of how old-fashioned this gesture was, but already she was imagining the graze of his lips on her skin, was anticipating the brush of his warm breath. But at the last moment he flipped her hand over so that his mouth pressed open and hot against her wrist.

Her pulse thundered into life under his molten kiss, her blood super-heated, melting her bones and stirring her dark, tender places into life. And as his liquid lips worked their magic on her skin and his tongue joined into the fray, ratcheting up the sensations another notch, she was certain that if he hadn't been holding on to her hand she might well have dissolved into a puddle on the floor.

She tasted as good as she looked. *Better*. This was going to be far more enjoyable than he would ever have anticipated.

And he had her. There was no question. The passion flaring into life in her eyes told him that she would be more than responsive, more than accom-

16

modating. The way her lips were softly parted told him she was eager for more of what his mouth could do for her, and the way her nipples pressed all too obviously against the tight fabric of her gown told him that even tonight would not be too soon.

She would soon be his. And then she would tell him everything she knew to save his sister.

And he would destroy Dr Della-Bosca and pull apart the clinic, even if he had to do it brick by brick!

He clamped down on the aching response of his own body as slowly, reluctantly, he drew his lips away.

'Who are you?' she asked, her words less a demand this time, more a breathy supplication.

He smiled and dipped his head fractionally, still with a hold on her hand. 'Loukas Demakis,' he said. 'A pleasure to meet you, Dr Ferraro.'

Her eyes narrowed and sparked, and he could see she was building connections as if suddenly understanding. Had the pieces fallen into place already? Had she realised the recently married Olympia was his sister? Did she have any idea at all why he was here?

'Demakis?' she repeated. 'As in the Senator currently making a run for the White House?'

'My father,' he replied, rapidly reassessing his quarry's intelligence. 'You've heard of him?'

Her eyes regarded him frostily as she tugged her hand out of his, using it to support her glass. 'Would that be such a surprise? I do try to keep informed of what's going on in the world around us. Did you assume that just because I spend my days working with beautiful people that I must be a complete airhead?'

'Not at all,' he countered. *Not any more.* 'I'd be a fool to make a mistake like that—obviously.'

She smiled a little then, a sweet smile of victory that didn't make it anywhere near her eyes. 'Obviously,' she mimicked, as if she knew damned well he'd underestimated her and been caught out.

His back teeth ground together. He certainly wouldn't do that again. There was much too much at stake to be outsmarted by any of Della-Bosca's cronies.

And that was all she was, he thought, forcing himself to remember, forcing himself to disregard the perfect skin and the womanly curves poured so skilfully into that dress. *One of Della-Bosca's cronies.* Regardless of the fact he still burned to possess her. Regardless of the fact he could already anticipate the feel of her honey-fleshed limbs around him.

And that last thought brought with it a smile as he flicked his gaze over her again. She would be good in bed—his own body's reaction told him that. There was no chance he'd misjudged her on that score.

He inhaled a steadying breath, finding it infused with her fragrance. Fresh. Spicy. Tempting.

'I'm sure my father will be gratified to hear his reputation extends so far.'

'Then be sure to tell him,' she replied. 'I'd actually like to see him make it all the way to the White House.'

He suppressed a snarl. Now what was she trying to prove? His father didn't need the support of people like her—people who did what she did, preying on the insecurity of others—and he certainly didn't want it.

'And you really care if he makes it?'

Her eyes narrowed and he felt their glacial challenge again.

'Is that so hard to believe?' she quipped, confirming his thoughts. 'I would have thought you'd be happy to find someone who supported your father's policy stance. Perhaps not. But, for what it's worth, I think there would be a kind of poetic justice in having someone like your father in the White House, don't you?'

His brow pulled tight. 'What do you mean?'

She arched an eyebrow and her blue eyes sparkled with confidence in a way that rankled. 'Given that ancient Greece was the cradle of democracy, I think there's a happy kind of irony there—democracy going full circle, if you like.' She paused, her wide mouth curling into a teasing smile that disappeared all too quickly.

'Besides, I've read about your father's background—how his grandparents arrived in the nineteen-twenties with nothing and yet built up a boat-building empire; it's a very impressive story. You must be very proud of your family's achievements.'

Was he? He hadn't thought about it or the business lately—he'd had more pressing things to think about, like his half-sister marrying an American reality TV programme loser, her love affair with celebrity, running with the brat-pack and screwing up her life, and a father who wanted her stopped before she screwed up his political aspirations or got herself killed—or both.

And he was going to make damned sure that didn't happen.

He looked down at her, his need to avenge the past and protect his sister setting his already heated blood to simmer point.

'Is that what you've got planned for yourself—your own rags to riches story?'

Her jaw worked from side to side as her eyes sparked cold flame.

'Excuse me, Mr Demakis. I'd really like to say it's been a pleasure...'

She turned to leave, a liquid ripple of blue disappearing into the crowd.

'So what's it like for an Australian in Beverly Hills?' he called after her through the babble and laughter of the crowded room.

She stopped dead, her back stiff, and then for a second it looked as if she was going to keep moving.

'What's it like to be so far from home?'

She swivelled this time, her expression perplexed. 'You picked up on my accent?' she said, moving closer. 'Most people don't.'

'It's there,' he lied, knowing that his knowledge of her country of birth had a great deal more to do with his research into her place in the Della-Bosca hierarchy than with any residual twang of an Australian accent.

She'd come to work at the clinic three years ago, obviously chasing the money and the high life it could provide her with. She'd hit pay-dirt right off, setting up with Della-Bosca and being swept along in her rise to celebrity and fortune. And now she was the successor to the throne. Nature's handmaiden in a world where beauty was paramount. Where fakery was king and no cost was too great.

'Why try to lose such a distinctive accent?' he asked, although he already knew the answer.

She shook her head, as if searching for a reason. 'It was too distinctive. It was easier to be accepted into society here without always answering questions about where I came from.' She shrugged. 'That's all.'

Fake, he thought. *Just like the rest of her.*

She looked up at him.

'Mr Demakis—' she began.

'Loukas,' he corrected, setting his voice to satin-smooth again. He'd wasted too much time, and he'd almost lost her once. It was time to take charge of the conversation again. 'Call me Loukas.'

She paused over that for a second, her top teeth gently raking over one glossy lower lip, almost as if the idea was strangely uncomfortable and needed to be come to terms with.

'Okay…Loukas,' she said finally, with a subtle nod of assent. 'What is it that brings you to the Saving Faces Foundation Gala? I can't remember your name on the guest list. Did you accompany someone here?'

He allowed himself a smile as he registered her continued interest. He hadn't lost her after all. She was still curious, still wanting to know more about him, still feeling the same physical tug of attraction that he felt too, and that would make his job that much easier. 'No. I came alone.'

Her head tilted fractionally. 'Then why are you here?'

'Just one reason,' he said, taking advantage of a passing waiter to rid her of her neglected glass. Then he took her right hand, lifting it until it was at her shoulder level between them before holding his palm flat against hers, interlacing their fingers together. He watched her widening eyes flit to their joined hands before finding his once more. 'But it's a very, very good one.'

'Oh?' she said, her voice a husky whisper, her blue eyes wary yet intrigued, her breathing but a shadow. 'And what might that be?'

Her faintly spicy feminine scent stirred his senses as his fingers curled between hers, and he drank in the woman before him. Blue eyes, high cheekbones, and a tendril of honey-coloured hair trailing loose from its sleek coil, kissing her neck wherever it touched in soft teasing waves.

His hunger built. That would soon be him, kissing the skin of her throat, kissing her slick, sweet lips, kissing every last inch of her until she cried out for release. And it would be no hardship to give it to her.

'Can't you tell?' he said as his free arm circled around her and he spun her with him onto the dance floor. 'I came here to meet you.'

It was the wrong answer.

His answer should have been couched in terms of wanting to support the foundation, of wanting to help children with shattered faces and fractured spirits to rebuild their lives and make them whole again. He should have been here to applaud the work of a great doctor and a worthy cause.

It was definitely not the answer she'd expected from a man who seemed dangerously threatening, at times resentful, and more often than not antagonistic. It wasn't the answer she'd wanted. He was hiding something behind those hard brown eyes, so shiny and impenetrable they might have been French polished. What was his real purpose? Why was he really here?

And yet, as he steered her expertly around the dance floor, his firm body an aching whisker from hers, somehow his words fed into her soul, fed those dark secret places until they pulsed into life. While her brain screamed to her that this was mad, that this was unwise, her body played a different tune.

Her body liked his words.

Her senses welcomed his message.

And her flesh wanted him closer still.

With each step he took her further away from the life she knew. With each whirl she felt inexorably, utterly, spun further away from her clinical—*practical*—medical background. In his arms she felt reckless, a little wild; she felt *good.*

He didn't speak, and she didn't mind. She doubted she could string two words together right now. Besides, she was too busy enjoying the unfamiliar sensations of being held by the best-looking man in the room.

His breath glided past her ear, soft and luxuriant, and she felt him draw her even closer. Her heart seemed to stop as their bodies met, the splayed hand at her waist forcing them into contact from chest to thigh, their movements on the dance floor setting up a sensual friction between them, his musky cologne like an invitation, beckoning her to nestle closer.

The music, the charged atmosphere, his body against hers—it was all so intoxicating. His lips nuzzled at her ear and she tilted her head into his caress, unashamedly seeking more of the warm, tingling contact he was offering.

'You're so beautiful,' he murmured softly, and the warm shimmer of sensation bloomed into a wave of heated sensuality that rolled over her and left her breathless.

She knew he was attracted to her, had sensed he was. His eyes contained secrets and mysteries, but his desire had broken through with a raw intensity that couldn't be ignored. And yet it was still such a powerful aphrodisiac to hear him say the words.

Everyone was beautiful here. There wasn't a woman there tonight whose looks didn't dazzle, whose bodies weren't centrefold-worthy, whose smiles weren't toothpaste-commercial-perfect. And yet, of all the women in the room, he'd said those words to her!

The hand at her waist stroked higher, breaching the low backline of her gown and startling her with its heated touch. He traced his fingers across her exposed skin, setting fires that burned with lightning bolt impact deep within her flesh and started spot fires low down inside.

The only part of logic that remained in her mind told her she was being seduced, that this was seduction at its most potent, and that this man was a master of the art. But, beyond that recognition, logic was no help to her now—not when she was being held captive by the spell he'd woven around her. Not when she was being swept off her feet.

'I want to make love to you.'

She gasped. His directness shocked at the same time as it delighted, sending coiled messages through her nerve-endings to prepare herself for coupling even before she'd had a chance to assimilate his offer.

What should she do? She could hardly take offence. Not when her own body hungered for the same outcome, was even now preparing itself, tingling with expectation.

His lips brushed over her earlobe and she raised her chin to give him better access. He took it, his mouth gliding over her throat, turning her nipples achingly tight.

Vaguely she was aware of the music drifting to a conclusion, of couples around them moving apart.

'Well?' he whispered in her ear, his deep voice another layer of seduction, another caress. 'Make love with me, Jade. Make love with me now—*tonight*.'

Something about the way he said her name wove its way deep into her senses, trailing a promise of things to come like a silken ribbon tugging insistently and irresistibly around her heated core.

He wanted to make love to her. To hear his words had sent her into a heady spin. Just the very thought of making love with this man was intoxicating. Because she knew what her body wanted. It wanted her to answer in the affirmative.

Was it wrong to want to? Was it wrong to want to give in to the desires that were besetting her? Wrong to give in to the forces of passion that were swirling around her—through her?

There should be one thousand reasons why not. There should be reasons clamouring for attention, pounding on her brain for supremacy. But right now none of them could be found, and rational thought was so heavily weighted with pure physical need that it threw up arguments instead about why she *should* make love with him. Arguments like, how could it possibly be wrong when it felt so damned right?

She lifted her head and looked into his eyes, felt the passion and the need, and knew that she couldn't bring herself to lie. She couldn't say no. And yet neither was she able to release herself totally from the constraints of her own upbringing. She'd never been the sort of person who did this sort of thing—meeting up with strangers and agreeing to make love with them.

And yet here she was...

'You're a very magnetic man,' she said, understating the facts by a factor of ten. 'And I admit I'm attracted...'

'But?' he urged.

'But I'm not protected,' she heard herself say—the most honest thing she could think of under the circumstances.

Something flared into life in his eyes, something that told her he wasn't disappointed at the naïveté of her confession, that his need was barely contained, let alone extinguished.

He let his arm peel slowly from around her back, instead winding it through hers and taking her hand as he led her from the floor. 'Allow me to take care of that.'

Despite the rush of cool air as they'd pulled apart, moist heat pooled heavy and insistent between her quivering thighs. Her heart thumping, she forced her legs to keep walking to the beat of the pounding in her veins, forced her melting spine to hold her erect.

He was leading her somewhere private. He was leading her somewhere to make love to her.

Her breath tripped in her throat. Had she meant to do that? Had her non-committal answer been designed to give him the chance to take the decision out of her hands? So that she would get what she wanted by default?

Somehow he negotiated her through the room. The strain of knowing she'd landed herself in this position was threatening to shatter the plastic smile masking her face; the anticipation of what was to come was urging her to move even faster. The crowd was thinning out, people were spilling out into the terraces, and by now there would no doubt be a pool full of skimpily clad young women offering their wares, ready to take on all comers.

Guests had drifted off into sheltered corners of the garden, or even not so sheltered ones, for their assignations. She'd never been comfortable with this side of celebrity life here in Beverly Hills—and yet wasn't that what she was now doing herself? Searching for privacy, seeking out what amounted to a love-nest with someone little more than a stranger? Did she really want to be doing this?

Whether he sensed her reluctance or was merely giving in to the relative quiet and darkness of a sheltered doorway some distance away, she found herself spun back against panelled wood as his mouth crashed down on hers.

His lips were warm, his mouth was hot, and what he did to her senses sent her temperature rocketing off the scale and forced any returning logic to flee. She'd never before been bombarded with sensations such as these, never before been subjected to the overwhelming drive of passion. And never before could have imagined herself giving in to it. But then, she'd had no idea...

His hands cupped her behind and she was pulled, full-length, up against his body, the clear evidence of his need pressing into her between them. She gasped into his mouth as she realised his evident size, felt his inherent power. Soon that power would be unleashed within her. She was melting down from the feel of his hands on her, from the touch of his lips, from the anticipation of what was to come.

He drew his head back the merest fraction, his breathing as ragged and choppy as hers. 'What's behind that door?' he said, his voice husky with desire, his words laced with need.

'The library,' she whispered back. 'But it should be locked.'

One hand left her for the moment it took to test the handle. It gave with the barest snick. Even in the gloom she could see the spark of his eyes gleaming down on her, as if he was closer to achieving some prize. Her heart fluttered as the realisation hit her. *She* was the prize. He wanted her and soon he would have her.

Instead of fear, her expectation cranked up another notch. This feeling was mutual. Because he wasn't the only one who was going to get something out of tonight.

Tonight she would have him too.

His lips came down to meet hers again, this time in a softer caress, his lips massaging hers, his tongue a brief graze across her teeth, and she let herself slide into his delicious touch. The man was good enough to eat, and she planned to relish every taste.

Loukas turned her then, and silently they slipped into the void opening up behind them. Gently he pressed her back against the wall. Softly he pushed the door closed alongside her. Another tiny snick, but another huge moment. Because that door closing meant that there was no changing her mind.

It meant there was no going back.

CHAPTER THREE

JADE let herself drown in the power of his kiss, giving herself up to his lips and his tongue and his raw masculine heat. Together they worked in a rhythm set by the primitive drumbeat pounding in her ears. He tasted so good—so right—and she answered his kiss with her own, seeking more, wanting more, her lips meshing with his, her tongue greedily seeking out whatever else he could give her.

She felt one arm circle her neck, pulling her closer to him. The other she felt skim across the skin of her back, setting off a zipper-line of sensation that started with the involuntary thrust of her hips against his and ended with her gasping into his mouth at what she encountered yet again.

His low, rumbling response told her he approved of her reaction, while his hand shifted to trace the underswell of her breast and then brushed over its surface, calling a halt to her breathing as it glanced over the nub of her tight nipple contained beneath.

And, like a jolt of electricity, panic seized her, breaking through the magic fog he'd spun around her, forcing rational thought to surface at last and finally find its rightful place in her mind. She hadn't thought this through! She hadn't been thinking, period.

What if he saw?

Why had she put herself in a position where she could be so thoroughly humiliated once again?

He'd said she was beautiful. Wasn't that enough for her? Couldn't she just have left it at that? She'd thought only of sex; she'd been too blinded by her own lust to see what should have been foremost in her mind: that Loukas would never want her when he knew. That Loukas would never in a million years think her beautiful once he knew.

His mouth was on her throat, his lips dancing a wild tango against her neck, and her heart was still racing. But now there was fear and trepidation in her mix of emotions.

She half registered a noise like a grunt, oddly distant when Loukas was so close. When the sound came again she froze.

Someone else was in the room.

She snapped her eyes open and peered over Loukas's shoulder. The pitch-blackness that had met them when they'd entered the large library had given way to a dim grey gloom in which nothing appeared to be moving or out of place between the walls of floor-to-ceiling books. She was imagining things. Against her throat Loukas's mouth continued to weave magic, complicating the push-pull of her fears and her wants as the sound came again.

Sounds.

In tune now with more than just the rush of blood in her ears, this time she heard a softer gasping moan answer the straining sounds. And more sounds, now louder, and more grunting, punctuated by urgent panting and then the unmistakable slap of flesh against flesh, building in speed, steadily and inexorably.

She squeezed her eyes shut again, wishing she could close down her hearing, afraid to breathe, afraid to move. Someone was making love—right here in the library—and they'd inadvertently stumbled right into their secret tryst.

But there was no shutting out what was happening, and the sounds fed into her consciousness, reminding her why *she'd* come there, and setting her flesh to prickling awareness of the man holding her even in her shock.

Because they'd come here to engage in that same act—to make those same noises, to seek that same inexorable release.

Loukas's mouth stilled and he pulled back as he too realised what was happening. He touched one finger to her lips and pulled her closer against him, as if sheltering her from what was happening while he edged a look over his shoulder. They had to get out of here. He would surely know that as well as she did. But before they could make a move a sound and a sudden movement in the low light drew her eyes directly to the source—and she found them.

Mostly hidden from view, sheltered from the door behind a long sofa, it was no wonder that whoever it was had been too absorbed to realise they had company. She was just about to turn her face away when the man rocked back on his knees and she recognised him.

Mayor Goldfinch!

No wonder the library door had been unlocked—Grace must have brought him here.

Now Jade had to get out, and take Loukas, before either of them saw her. She would never in a million years subject Grace to that kind of embarrassment.

She couldn't let her find out that they had inadvertently stumbled upon them during such a private act.

She prodded Loukas to leave, but he stilled her movements. 'Wait,' he whispered, so quietly she half wondered if she'd inhaled his words instead. 'Wait just a moment.'

But she didn't want to stay. She didn't want to hear any more, to be witness to anyone's lovemaking—least of all to Grace's. More than anything she wanted to get out, now, and it took supreme strength of will to remain cradled in Loukas's arms while she waited seemingly for ever for the pair to resume their frantic activities.

The sounds of motion and mounting excitement finally resumed, telling her Mayor Goldfinch had Grace exactly where he wanted her once more. She wanted to close her ears as every sound, every whimper, fed into her own needs, making her overwhelmingly aware of what she herself might be doing right now, of what she'd given her tacit agreement to. Her flesh shimmied into action where Loukas held her, where she brushed up alongside him, as the aura of coupling wrapped itself around them.

But at last they were moving out of here. Loukas was just manoeuvring her closer to the door, ready to bundle her out, when she heard gruff words.

'Oh, Rach. Oh, sweet baby, I've missed you.'

For a second she thought she'd misheard the name—it had to have been Grace that he'd said—but then she spied the lush sheen of red satin slung over the settee, had recognised the young, drawling tones responding enthusiastically to the Mayor's encouragement and cold revulsion worked its clammy way up her spine.

Because it wasn't Grace that Mayor Goldfinch was entertaining. It was Rachael Delaney!

She almost cried out with the shock, but a large firm hand clamped down over her mouth, rendering her mute. Under cover of the noise of the couple's latest activities, Loukas had the door pulled open and whisked her back outside before she could react—and before the couple could know what was happening.

She burst free from his grip and threw herself along the passageway, gulping in great mouthfuls of air, trying to clear her lungs of the filth of that room.

'Jade!' she heard him call. 'Jade!'

She couldn't answer—wouldn't stop as she fled. She wanted to go upstairs to her suite but, knowing Loukas might follow her, she made for the safety of the crowded ballroom. Did Grace have any idea the man she was hoping would propose was busy slaking his lust on one of her guests? Did she have any idea the man she was hoping to marry was such a low-class act?

She had to get away. Away from the betrayal going on behind her. Away from the cheap act that she herself had been about to take part in.

Loukas had said he wanted to make love to her, and she'd let herself be swept away—yet it wasn't *love* that people made in secret trysts like the one they'd just happened upon. There was no love involved. It was just sex—pure, unadulterated animal lust—and she'd just about let herself cave into the same base desires.

She felt sick to the stomach.

A steel band took hold of her arm, wheeling her around. 'Stop.'

She looked up into his eyes, wanting but unable to contain her desperate need for oxygen.

'Let me go,' she insisted.

'You were happy for me to touch you before.'

'That was before. I'm sorry. I made a mistake. I should never have gone with you. I should never have led you on like that.'

'You didn't lead me on. We both wanted to make love. Still want to make love. You can't deny that.'

'No,' she said, shaking her head wildly, as if to shake out the soiled images and damning sounds that replayed endlessly through her mind. 'Not like that. That wasn't love that was being made in there. I was wrong. I'm sorry.'

'Come with me, then. We'll get out of this rats' nest and talk.'

'No.' She held one hand up as she backed away. Her skin burned with both humiliation and embarrassment. It was bad enough having lived through the experience without having to analyse it. 'I'm sorry, Mr Demakis. There's nothing to talk about.' Then she turned and fled into the ballroom.

'This isn't over!'

There was no point arguing with him; she just kept right on surging away from him. He'd picked the wrong woman, that was all. No more explanations necessary.

If it was just quick sex he was after she had no doubt he'd find someone else for the night—a woman who would be more accommodating and who had less hang-ups, who wouldn't be fazed about sharing a room with another couple hard at it, a woman who would happily look elsewhere if she was in that situation. And there was every chance he'd find that woman here.

With his looks he'd have his pick. And she'd almost fallen for him—hook, line and sinker. To think he'd swayed her so much with that line of his—*'I came here to meet you.'* She'd played right into his hands. Thank God she'd had enough sense not to take him upstairs to her suite—there would have been no escape then.

No, he'd find someone else in short order, and there was no chance she'd ever see Mr Loukas Demakis again.

The rush of relief she felt at that prospect evaporated the instant she noticed the last person she wanted to talk to right now heading straight for her.

'Oh, Jade,' Grace said, casting her eyes all about the room. 'You haven't seen Mayor Goldfinch anywhere?'

Jade stood blankly, her stomach lurching as she fought to raise her eyes above shoe level.

'Only I wanted to show him the clinic's latest plans for expansion, and he seems to have disappeared.'

'I can't help you,' Jade insisted, her heart breaking for the older woman even as she lied. Grace would have to find out the truth at some time, but not now. Jade couldn't bear to spoil her otherwise perfect night. 'Have you tried the garden?' she added, taking her by the arm and steering her towards the French doors to ensure she couldn't stumble into the library and discover the Mayor's sleazy betrayal herself. Because while half of her wanted Grace to find out what kind of man he really was, the other half wanted to protect her friend from the pain of knowing the whole sordid truth. 'I'll help you look.'

The young girl looked up, her kohl-rimmed eyes hopeful and expectant as Jade entered the consulting room. While outwardly Jade acknowledged both Grace and the client, inwardly she sighed. Despite the heavy make-up, Jade knew the young waif-like blonde was barely eighteen years old—and yet already Pia Kovac was a regular customer at the clinic—too regular for her liking.

'Thanks for stepping in, Dr Ferraro,' said Grace. 'Pia has asked us to consider doing a few extra little things for her. Seeing as a couple of them will require your deft touch with the laser, I thought you should sit in on this consultation.'

'No problem,' Jade responded, taking a seat in one of the velvet sofas surrounding the plush coffee table set-up when what she really wanted was to go back to her apartment at the mansion and let herself slip into a long soaking bath.

How did Grace do it? She looked at her now, as she outlined the procedures Pia had in mind, and could only marvel at how fresh and bright-eyed she looked even while she still managed to retain an air of serenity and calm about her. No doubt about it— the woman was amazing. Jade would be up to her neck in bubbles right now if she hadn't been called in to this consultation.

Today had been too long—a full day of laser surgery punctuated only by an hour-long luncheon meeting with Grace to discuss the financial results from the Gala.

As expected, the evening had been a runaway success in raising both funds and the profile of the foundation. Months of planning had paid off, and Jade was now feeling the anticlimax of masterminding and carrying off a successful event seeping through her bones.

But that wasn't the only anticlimax she was feeling. Ever since that night she'd felt strangely let down, and it all had to do with the larger-than-life memories of one tall, dark stranger. And yet nothing had happened between them, really. Nothing compared to what might have happened. Right now she could be filled with regrets about crazy actions and impetuous desires. She could be cursing herself for giving in to nothing more than base lust.

Instead she should feel proud of herself for having had the strength to get out of the situation. She should be feeling relieved she'd come to her senses before it was too late—even if it had taken a philandering mayor to wake her up to what she was doing.

So why did she feel as if she'd missed out? Why was she disappointed that she'd heard not a thing from Loukas Demakis when it was clearly to her advantage never to run into the man again?

With a struggle she forced her could-have-been lover out of her mind and brought her focus back to the shopping basket of cosmetic goodies Grace was outlining. It was an impressive list; Pia had obviously been doing her homework.

'Jade,' Grace said at last, 'would you agree that's the best way to proceed? For you to do the minor laser surgery components before I've done the breast augmentation?'

Jade drew in a weary breath and looked at the young woman sitting opposite—a teenager, certainly, but hardly flat-chested. She suppressed a sigh. This was one of the things that really grated about this business. It was one thing for the clinic to be helping people retain or reclaim their youthful looks, but it seemed another thing entirely to start with major re-modelling of the looks of someone barely out of puberty.

'Pia,' she said gently, 'are you sure you've thought this all through? A breast augmentation isn't something to take lightly. Are you sure you really need it?'

Pia's expression dropped like a stone. 'But I have to do something. Kurt says the only thing wrong with me is I don't have enough up top.'

Jade glanced over her notes. 'Then why the liposuction?'

'Kurt hates fat.'

It was hardly a surprising answer. Kurt hadn't liked her nose or her lips either, when Pia had first appeared on the clinic's doorstep six months ago, a newlywed with a massive inferiority complex and a demanding would-be celebrity husband. Without a doubt the failed reality TV contender had had more than a little to do with her recent cheek implants as well.

'And what do you like? What do you really want, Pia?'

'I want to keep Kurt.' Her words came out like a sulky child threatened with the loss of her favourite bedtime toy. Which was probably how she felt, given the rumours that Kurt was already tiring of his hastily arranged Las Vegas marriage.

'And of course you will,' crooned Grace, sending daggers to Jade as she shifted next to Pia on the couch, taking her hand and stroking it gently. 'And we'll do everything to help you. Won't we, Jade?'

'What was that all about?'

Jade was just collecting her purse and jacket when Grace paced purposefully into her office. 'It sounded very much like you were trying to talk Pia *out* of surgery back there.'

Jade rubbed her brow and tucked a stray strand of hair behind her ear. 'I'm sorry, Grace. I just think she's too young to be doing all this. Especially when she doesn't need it. If it wasn't for Kurt—'

'Kurt's her husband. Of course she wants to please him! Our job is to give the clients what they want. Not to talk them out of it.'

'But she's so young—'

'She won't be young for ever. Satisfy her now and we'll have a client for life.' She arched one eyebrow high, accentuating her bright eyes. 'Think about that. Your future is with people just like Pia. Sow the seeds now, and reap the harvest for life.'

Jade recoiled at her words. When had Grace become so cynical?

'I didn't think the clinic was so desperate for money that we had to go recruiting teenagers.'

'She came to us. We didn't "recruit" her. And don't sniff at the money. It pays you well enough, doesn't it? I've tried to make you feel welcome here, and I've tried to support you while you become established. Haven't I opened my home up to you, giving you your own space? I thought you enjoyed working here,' she continued. 'I thought we were part of a team. But then, if you're not happy...'

The older woman's eyes clouded over suddenly, and her unfinished sentence was enough to sting Jade with remorse.

Grace was right, of course. Grace was more like a fairy godmother than a colleague—making her dreams come true not just once in her life, but twice.

Because it had been Grace's removal of her ugly facial birthmark that had given Jade the inspiration and the courage to enter the same field and pursue the quest for excellence. She wanted the chance to make such amazing differences to other people's lives too. She wanted the chance to put something back. And Grace had given her that opportunity too, when she'd approved her application and given her a place at the clinic.

She owed *everything* to Grace—her job, her success, and most of all the chance to be accepted as a normal human being. Nobody had ever done so much for her. Nobody else had made her life so worthwhile.

So Jade wouldn't let her down—especially not now, when it was clear that Grace was already in for a rough ride when she discovered the truth about Mayor Goldfinch.

'I'm sorry,' she said. 'Of course I'm happy working here.'

'Then don't let me hear any more about you trying to talk people out of surgery. You have a gift, and these people need you. They'll do anything to look better.' Grace reached out and grasped her forearm, squeezing it so hard her acrylic nails bit deep into Jade's flesh. 'You, more than anyone, should appreciate that.'

She'd been so close. If he'd taken her somewhere else, if he'd found somewhere private, she would have been his. Even now, leaning against the door of her champagne-coloured Mercedes convertible in the palm-tree-lined car park behind the Della-Bosca Clinic, he could still feel her in his arms, feel her shuddering response to his touch.

She'd wanted him that night!

She'd melted into his arms like warm syrup and he could have had her. If it hadn't been for the Mayor and his young bimbo beating them to it, he would have had her. She'd been his for the taking. Ripe and luscious and so hot to touch that he was aching to have another chance to unleash the passion he knew was lurking beneath that polished exterior.

He smiled to himself as he pocketed his sunglasses. If she thought her rapid departure meant she'd escaped him, she had another think coming. He wasn't done with this strategy just yet.

So far he'd accomplished none of the things he'd set out to do to comply with his father's request to keep his sister safe; he'd found out none of the information he needed to pull the rug out from underneath Dr Della-Bosca's Manolo-clad feet. But there was still no better way to find out what he needed to than to coax it out of her young colleague.

And next time he'd make sure there was no chance for her to change her mind. Next time she wouldn't get away.

His body hummed with anticipation of the hunt. The information couldn't come more enticingly gift-wrapped. The idea of extracting what he needed to know couldn't possibly give him more of a charge.

She might be as plastic as the industry she worked for, and the celebrities she practised on, but at least she was making his quest more entertaining than he'd ever imagined possible.

He pulled one hand from his pocket and glanced down at his watch, but it only confirmed what the sun was already telling him as it dipped lower in the sky—the doctor kept long hours. The nip and tuck business was obviously booming.

Then a movement at the side door caught his eye. It was her. As she stepped from the door her hand went to the back of her head, and with a toss she pulled a clip from her hair, releasing it. He growled his approval as the wave swung around her face and tumbled over her shoulders like a sweep of honey.

He liked the way she looked with her hair down. Even more than how it looked, it appealed to his sense of economy.

One less thing for him to remove.

She couldn't wait to get into that bath. Grace might be content to stay and deal with paperwork till all hours, but Jade had had enough for one day. And there was absolutely no need for Grace to stay back. They had enough staff that Grace need never bother herself with administration, but she'd always been hands-on, always been involved, even with matters as mundane as the accounts. She was a total inspiration.

Her neck and shoulders aching, Jade unclipped her hair as she stepped from the building, already men-

tally unwinding as she shook her hair free. She took
two steps into the car park and froze.

It was him. He was leaning against her car and
looking for all the world as if he owned it. Did he
know it was hers? In the same instant she asked herself the question she'd already answered herself in the
affirmative. Of course he knew. Why else would he
be sprawled all over it? How he knew wasn't even
an issue. This man didn't strike her as the sort who
would have trouble getting anything—least of all information.

But what the hell was he doing here? Even in the
gathering twilight the foolishness of her actions at the
ball came back in stark detail to taunt her. And she
didn't want to be reminded of that night. Didn't want
to be reminded of what had nearly happened. Didn't
want to be reminded of how his firm body and his
sultry mouth had made her feel...

She swallowed down an urge to turn around and
walk the other way. She'd run from him once before,
and be damned if he'd see her bolt again. It was her
car he was leaning on. He was the one who was going
to leave.

So she forced her legs to move once more, forced
herself closer to where he stood so casually regarding
her approach, his hands in his pockets, one leg bent
over the other, while she wound tighter and tighter
inside like a coiled spring.

She stopped two metres shy, wondering how the
hell she was going to get into her car while he leaned
against her door.

She nodded. 'Mr Demakis.'

'Loukas,' he corrected. 'How are you, Dr Ferraro?'

If he thought that was an invitation to ask him to call her Jade he was very much mistaken. 'You seem to be blocking my car door.'

He looked around as if surprised. 'This is your car? Now, there's a coincidence.'

'An unbelievable coincidence, I would have thought,' she said, making it clear she knew it was no accident of fate that had brought them together today.

'It seems we have a mutual liking for this particular marque,' he continued, indicating the car alongside hers. Another sleek Mercedes Sports, although so clearly the top of the line it made her smaller soft-top look like a basic city run-around. 'I wonder what else we have in common?'

His easy banter grated on her nerves, especially as his eyes gave her different messages entirely. In what remained of the light of day they were nowhere near as dark as they'd seemed in the evening lighting, more a rich chestnut colour—though right now they contained a noticeable absence of warmth. And yet she felt a heat emanating from them that burned into her senses and touched parts of her deep down inside, where the humming his touch had set in train Saturday evening was coming alive once again.

How could he do that? Look so cold and imperious in the same instant he was setting her skin aflame?

She shifted her stance, trying to quell her mutinous flesh and disguising her purpose by digging through her purse for her keys.

'Who can say?' She took a step closer, holding her keys pointedly. 'Now, if you'll excuse me?'

He didn't move an inch, still leaning against the

car door, and she was left wondering about the wisdom of moving closer to him.

'You're not curious enough to find out?'

She tilted her head up to his face, taking in the challenging glint in his eyes and the crooked smile. Why was he here? Did he see her as an easy target? Did he expect her to fall into bed with him the moment he reappeared in her life and take up where they'd left off in the library?

Or was there just the remotest chance he was really interested in getting to know her?

Oh, yes, she was curious all right. And it had nothing to do with what they had or didn't have in common. But, whatever he wanted, there was no chance she'd be swept away by irrationality again. Once was more than enough.

And, if he was honestly interested in getting to know her better, he'd soon work out that ambushing someone in the car park after a long day was hardly the way to win friends.

She forced what she hoped would pass as a smile to her face. 'Not in the least bit curious,' she lied. 'And I really have to be leaving now, so if you'll kindly sprawl over your own car instead, I'll get going.'

He laughed out loud, pushing himself upright, away from her car. *At last,* she thought, sensing escape was near at hand. But still he didn't move his feet. And now he was even closer. Close enough to bring memories of that night, of being next to his body, held by his arms against his muscled torso, crashing over her. Close enough that if she just reached out her hand she could once again touch him, could feel his heated skin through her fingertips, feel the beat of his heart pulse its way into hers.

'Are all Australian women as refreshingly direct as you?'

His words broke into her consciousness, snapping her out of the crackling tension of her imagination. What the hell was she thinking? Another moment and she would have been imagining tumbling *him* into bed. She had to get out of here, and fast.

She raised her chin. 'Are all sons of Greek success stories as frustratingly obstinate as you? I asked you very politely to get out of the way.'

He stood surveying her for what seemed like for ever, his brown eyes frosted and unreadable, a twitching muscle in his jaw his only movement. Finally, when she'd all but given up hope of ever getting into her vehicle and was contemplating hailing a cab instead, he suddenly moved to his left. It gave her enough room to pull the wide door open, but not enough to ensure she wouldn't have to brush past him as she sat down in the driver's seat. But it would have to do.

She stepped forward, hoping to get by as quickly as possible, steeling herself against the prickle of sensation that she knew would come with passing so close to him.

'You haven't even asked me why I'm here,' he said, once she was safely in her seat.

'You've had more than enough opportunity to tell me,' she replied, turning the key in the ignition and gunning the engine for effect.

He hunkered down alongside her, ignoring her blatant desire to get out of there as quickly as possible,

one elbow resting on the window, the other above her
on the roof and his face perilously close to her own.
Instead of feeling in a position of strength, suddenly
sitting down in the car made her feel more vulnerable
than ever. He dwarfed the sports coupé's entry, his
limbs spread wide like a spider about to encompass
its prey.

'So humour me for one more minute,' he urged,
his warm, masculine scent beckoning like a drug. She
could almost feel herself being drawn further and further into his web. 'Let me explain why I'm here.'

Her eyes looked longingly through the windscreen
to the car park exit and the main road beyond, her
hands grimly clawed on the leather-covered steering
wheel. She was so close to escape, so close to getting
away. But would one minute matter? Why not let him
say what he wanted to? Then she could be out of here.
Then she would be able to think straight again.

'Okay,' she said on a resigned sigh. 'You've got
one minute. Why are you here? What do you want?'

'I want you to come to dinner with me.'

Her skin goosebumped at the unexpected invitation. *Dinner.* It was a harmless enough concept, so
why did she feel as if she herself was on the menu?
After how close they'd come at the ball, would he be
expecting her to move from the dining room to the
bedroom with no hesitation? And would he be right?
She bit down on her lip. Whatever her reservations,
whatever her sense that there was more to this man
than he revealed, the thought of following through on
what she'd missed out on was more than tempting.

She'd certainly thought about it quite enough in the
intervening days since the party—thought about what

it would have been like to make love to this man, what it would have felt like to have him inside her. Would the reality come anywhere near the fantasy? Or would the real man surpass the man in her dreams?

She sucked in air, clamping down on her desires and on the spreading warmth between her thighs. It couldn't happen. She'd had a fortunate escape once already. She'd almost made a total fool of herself and only just saved herself from certain humiliation. She couldn't expect her luck to hold out a second time.

'I'm sorry,' she said, reaching past him for the handle to pull closed her door. 'I'm busy tonight.' *Washing my hair.*

'Then make it tomorrow night.'

She swallowed. 'I really don't think that's such a good idea. I'm sorry you've wasted your time.'

He didn't take the hint, instead remaining exactly where he was. 'My minute isn't up yet. And I think you really do want to accept my invitation.'

'Why on earth would I want to do that?' she snapped, her patience worn thin.

'Because it's attached to a one-million-dollar donation to the foundation—that's why.'

CHAPTER FOUR

THE disbelief must have been evident in her eyes even as her hand dropped from the door. Benefactors on such a scale were notoriously thin on the ground. They didn't usually just fall into your lap like a ripe peach, without a great deal of time and effort spent shaking the tree. *One million dollars.* That kind of money would give a mighty kickstart to the foundation's new overseas children's assistance programme. And he was offering the foundation that just to eat with him!

Or was he?

'Let me get this straight—you'll give one million dollars to the foundation and all I have to do is have dinner with you?'

'As simple as that.'

Nothing was that simple. Not in this town. She raised an eyebrow.

'Are you trying to buy me, Mr Demakis?'

'I said you could call me Loukas.'

'You haven't answered my question.'

'I'm trying to make a contribution to the wonderful work of your foundation. Nothing more.'

'So this isn't some underhanded way of finishing what you started Saturday night?'

His head tilted, his eyebrows rising in speculation.

'Is that what you're hoping?'

Breath lurched inwards through her teeth, and she

could only hope her cheeks weren't betraying the sudden rush of heat to her skin. 'I think you misunderstand me. I just need us both to be clear on this. I'm not interested in taking your money if there are certain strings attached.'

He paused a moment. 'Do you really think I would pay one million dollars for what I could have had for free?'

Her eyelids fell shut as his words doused her in a cold dose of reality. Of course he was right. Why would he imagine he'd have to pay that kind of money for her? She'd shown how cheaply she could be bought when she'd been right there in that room with him.

Her eyes started open at the touch of his fingers as they drew her chin around to face him. 'You shouldn't take that the wrong way,' he said.

Heart thumping wildly in her chest, she searched his brown eyes for meaning. What other way was there to take his words? But she didn't have to say a thing. She knew the question was right there in her eyes.

'When you make love to me,' he said, his voice washing over her like rich velvet, 'it won't be because I have to pay you. It will be because you want to.'

She swallowed, her mind battling to grab hold of logic and rationality in the sea of foaming sensation bubbling inside.

'*When* you make love to me' he'd said. Not *if*.

Part of her wanted to argue—who was this man to presume to know what she wanted?—while another part of her recognised the simple truth at the core of his assertion. Because there was something about this man—something that drew her closer and more intensely than any man she'd ever met. And whether it was merely lust or a powerful attraction or something else that was driving her thoughts, simply knowing that eventually, ultimately, they would make love gave her flesh a shivery tingle of anticipation.

At last she managed to unknot her tongue enough to respond. 'You sound very sure of yourself, Mr Demakis.'

'Oh,' he said, holding her chin steady as he angled himself closer, 'it's not just me I'm sure about.'

His lips met hers in more of a tingle than a meeting of flesh. He was there, barely touching, so she could sense his contact rather than feel it. His low breathing fanning her face, mingling with hers. And waiting for more was like exquisite torture.

Her earlier weariness was shrugged off. Every part of her now felt alive, sparkling, *special*. And when his lips brushed over hers and closed that final millimetre she knew why she'd felt lucky to have escaped Loukas's influence before. Because she didn't think she could escape if she tried. Even worse, she knew she wouldn't try to. Because right now there was nowhere she'd rather be.

If there was such a thing as a perfect fit, she was sure she'd found it. His lips wove sweet magic over hers in a tender caress that felt as if it was made for her and her alone. She heard a noise, a strangely foreign sigh that sounded like someone slipping into ecstasy, only to register with surprise that it had come from her. She was the one slipping away.

And then all of a sudden his lips were withdrawing, and she knew that whatever arguments she put up about not wanting to sleep with him would be rendered completely useless after that kiss. No matter what she said, what she claimed to the contrary, there was no way he wouldn't know she was completely and utterly his for the taking. There was no way he wouldn't know it was only a matter of time.

She opened her eyes hesitantly, unsteadily, almost afraid to meet his eyes because of how they might look—smug?—victorious?

But his hand continued to cup her chin, and there was no option but to raise her lashes and look up at him. What she saw there was even more disconcerting than his kiss. Because there was arrogance, there was even a kind of victory, but there was confusion and questions too—questions that swirled and eddied and muddied the depths of those brown eyes, questions that she couldn't begin to understand, let alone answer.

Yet there was one question she could answer—right now.

'Yes,' she said, running her tongue over her lips, tasting the essence of him on her skin.

His brows pulled together. 'Yes what?'

'Yes.' *To anything you want.* 'If it means one million dollars for the foundation, I'll have dinner with you.'

'I don't know, Grace. I can't put my finger on what it is that's bothering me, but it doesn't seem right somehow.' Jade stopped pacing the living room long enough to rest her hands on the back of one of the soft peach-coloured sofas while Grace sat opposite, sipping on her post-supper coffee.

Ever since she'd become aware Grace had arrived home from the clinic, Jade had been itching to talk to her about Loukas and his planned contribution. After their friction today she'd wanted to share the good news—although now she wasn't so sure it *was* good news.

At least, not for her.

'You can't be having second thoughts,' said Grace practically. 'You've already told him you'd go.'

Jade looked down at her hands, steadily working indentations into the soft leather. 'I could always tell him I made a mistake—that I've changed my mind. Maybe he'll give the money anyway.'

'Change your mind and risk losing me one million dollars? No, you will not! You'll go to dinner like you agreed.'

Jade looked up suddenly. 'It's not for you, Grace, it's for the foundation.'

'Ah, but,' she said, replacing her drained bone china cup onto its saucer with barely a click, 'who is it who supports the foundation if there are insufficient funds? The clinic.' She pointed one tapered red fingernail at her chest. 'Meaning me.'

'But the foundation has plenty of capital. The Gala alone must have set us up for two years of operation. I can't see you having to bail it out any time soon.'

Grace held up one hand. 'All the same, Jade, if something does happen, it's me who will have to foot the bill. That million dollars will be a welcome buffer, given the clinic has had a few unforeseen expenses lately.'

Jade's ears pricked up. 'You haven't mentioned this before. What kind of expenses?'

'Oh, I wasn't going to bother you with any of this. They're just annoying little things, really—one or two little cases. Someone who wants to sue me in some ridiculous claim to do with their surgery, somebody else claiming negligence—and the lawyers want me to go for settlements.'

'*More* cases?' Jade side-stepped the sofa and sat down alongside Grace. 'Oh, how awful for you. They must think you're an easy target. Maybe just for once you should go to court—fight them this time. It can't be good if you always settle—people will learn to expect a pay-out for everything.'

Grace patted her hand. 'Thank you. I insisted we fight too! But the lawyers think it's best to keep everything as quiet as possible. They don't want the clinic brought up in court—they think it would be bad publicity all round.' She shrugged. 'And, seeing they're the experts, I can't really argue with them.'

'But if it means always shelling out money to make these people go away, how long can you continue doing business that way? And what will it mean for the expansion plans for the clinic? Will they still go ahead?'

'Oh, yes. But only with the Mayor's help. He's agreed to take over the building contract and give us a good deal. I'm just so lucky he's standing by me through all of this. I really don't know what I'd do without him.'

Every muscle and organ inside Jade seemed to clench and roll at the mention of that word. Why couldn't he just leave Grace alone? She was going to end up hurt, and badly, when she found out what the Mayor was really like. And now she was tying herself

to him for a year or more while the contract works
were carried out.

Grace would have to discover the truth for herself
at some stage. Or was Jade going to have to tell her?

'Maybe you should put it off for a while?' Jade
suggested tentatively. 'Maybe wait until these cases
are cleared up and out the way before you commit to
any more expenditure.' *And to the Mayor.*

'Oh, there's no need for that. It's all organised—
the Mayor's taken care of all that. Now, before I head
off to bath and bed, I want to know—you *are* going
to that dinner tomorrow night?'

She sighed. 'I don't know, Grace. I'm not even sure
I believe him. If he'd wanted to give the foundation
a cheque for so much money, why didn't he tell us
at the Gala? We could have announced it then and
there. Why wait until afterwards?'

Grace shrugged as she stood up. 'If he's willing to
donate that much money, let him set the conditions.
It's only dinner after all.' She looked down, her eyes
shrewd, to where the younger woman was still sitting.
'Or do you think he expects more for his money than
just dinner? Are you worried he wants to sleep with
you?'

Jade felt herself colour. Not so much because of
the question but more at Loukas's words, playing
over and over in her mind in stark and brutal relief.
*Do you really think I would pay one million dollars
for what I could have had for free?*

She swallowed, dropping her eyes. 'He assured me
it was just dinner.'

'Then you have nothing at all to worry about. And,
let's face it, it's only if he expects you to take your

clothes off and he sees your scars that you have a problem. We don't want him asking for his money back, do we?'

'Do you miss your home?'

Jade sipped on her margarita and stared out through the windows of the restaurant at the end of the pier, down past the fair rides and stalls to the row of lights marking out the Santa Monica Bay shoreline.

When she'd agreed to dinner she'd never expected Loukas to bring her to a place like this—so relaxed and unpretentious. She was glad he had—the casual surroundings and the margarita had woven a mellow spell over her, making it easier to talk. At least until he'd asked her about her home.

Her eyes followed the line of lights down the coast to where they disappeared into the sea mist and the smog. It was so different here compared to the small rural town of Yarrabee where she'd grown up—five hours and a world away from Sydney and the sea, where everything and everyone, the crops, the livestock, even life itself, seemed ruled by the seasons and the weather.

Unless you didn't fit in.

Then your life revolved around avoiding people, staring at the ground and, just like everyone else around you, wishing you'd never been born.

Absence was supposed to make the heart grow fonder but even after her self-imposed exile it was impossible to conjure up any feelings of sentiment for the place. Yarrabee had made her feel like an outcast from the beginning. And now just thinking about Yarrabee left her cold. Because how could a place that had never wanted you ever be considered your home?

Even Sydney, to where she'd escaped at last for medical school, didn't feel like home to her now. Maybe because there was no one waiting for her back there. No one she'd left behind.

She looked around, saw Loukas staring, waiting for her reply.

'Miss home? Not really,' she admitted, brightening her smile with more warmth than she felt. 'I've swapped Aussie sunshine for the Californian variety. I've made my home here now, and I'm happy with that decision.'

As easily as that! Did she realise how her smoothly delivered words condemned her, reminding him in no uncertain terms just what kind of woman she was? She'd transplanted herself smack-bang into a lucrative industry in the most body-conscious city in North America. Didn't she have any feelings for those she must have left behind? What kind of woman was she?

'What about your family?' he insisted, thinking of his father and how even now that Olympia was married he still wanted to control her life and keep her safe. 'How do they feel about you being so far away?'

She shook her head. 'I guess I'm lucky in that respect. I don't have any family to worry about.'

For the first time he felt there was more to her easy dismissal of her homeland than she'd let on. Not having a family seemed a strange thing to consider yourself lucky about.

'What happened to them?'

She screwed up her face and sat back in her chair. 'Look, you don't want to hear all this. It's history.'

'Humour me.'

She blinked and looked at him, her blue eyes

clearly weighing up whether or not to talk. In the end she took a deep gulp of air and shrugged, almost as if telling him that he'd asked for it. 'There's not a lot to it. My mother died when I was born. All I know of her I've learned from photographs.'

'She must have been very beautiful.'

A bright smile lit up her face, so brilliant and yet so brief. But he could tell from her eyes that the smile wasn't directed at him. She was looking inwards, remembering. 'Would you believe,' she said, 'she was actually Miss Yarrabee Showgirl the year she turned seventeen?'

'Yeah,' he said, acknowledging that, whatever cosmetic surgery Jade had been treated to while at the Della-Bosca Clinic, she must have started out with some pretty decent genes in the first place. 'I'd believe it. And I'd believe it more if you told me you'd followed suit.'

Her smile faded and she blinked as her focus briefly settled back on him before she let her gaze fall to the table. And when her voice came it was as if her words were hidden by shadows, heavy with ghosts.

'No, I never entered.'

He watched her study her margarita as she swirled the contents around the glass, tickling the salt-encrusted rim, slowly dissolving it. Before the past had intervened in her thoughts her face had shone with an unparalleled brilliance. What would it take for her to direct that dazzling smile onto him and mean it? Could you seduce someone into smiling like that? He was aching to try. But she was in the mood to talk, and anything she told him was going to help his cause.

'So how old were you when your father died?'

'Heaps older, thankfully. Fifteen.'

'How did it happen?'

She nodded matter-of-factly, obviously having anticipated his question. 'We had a small spread outside Yarrabee. One night he didn't come home for dinner and I went looking for him. I thought maybe the old tractor had broken down again—he was always complaining that he'd have to get a decent one some time, but we could never quite afford it.'

She paused, her gaze fixed on a point somewhere out on the horizon.

'You found him?'

She nodded, bringing her blank gaze back down to her drink.

'The tractor had rolled down an embankment. Dad was pinned underneath. He was still alive when I found him. He could talk—told me it didn't hurt too badly and to go get help. I told him it would be all right. I told him to hang on while I ran to get help and I'd be back as soon as I could. He told me he'd hang on...'

Silence stretched out between them, long and strained.

Finally she breathed in deeply, her face tilting apologetically, though signs of strain still clung to her eyes. 'I'm sorry. Way too much information.'

'No,' he insisted, realising his feelings of compassion were surprisingly genuine. He reached out a hand, loosening hers from the side of her glass, squeezing her fingers within his. 'I'm sorry. I shouldn't have asked.'

'It's okay. Really,' she said, making no effort to remove her hand. He let his thumb stroke her fingers, a gentle massage that reminded him of how good she felt in his arms and made him realise how much he was looking forward to holding her again.

'So now you have no family?'

She dipped her head—a silent assent. 'But I've been lucky too,' she said. 'Grace has been very good to me—taking me on board, inviting me to share her house. She's the closest thing I have to family now.'

Everything inside him shut down. His thumb ceased its stroking as resentment simmered to the surface at the mention of that name. Any compassion he had felt for a young girl who had suffered the loss of both her mother and her father in tragic circumstances dissolved in the acid burn of his hatred for all things Della-Bosca.

This woman sitting opposite him was no innocent. She was part of Della-Bosca's evil web. She was part of the problem and he had better not forget it.

'Loukas?'

Her blue eyes held concern—concern for him. It was ironic. She wouldn't look that way if she knew what he had planned for her precious Dr Della-Bosca. But first he needed her help. First he needed hard evidence. And, above all, he needed to ensure the safety of his half-sister.

He smiled then, as he forced the rancid ball of his hatred deep down inside himself again. 'But that's not all, Jade,' he said, giving her hand a reassuring squeeze. 'Now you have me too.'

*   *   *

Something had changed between them tonight. As they strolled hand in hand down the length of the pier, neither of them talking, Jade knew that whatever relationship they shared had moved to a new level. And it had nothing whatsoever to do with his promise of a one-million-dollar donation.

Her body hummed with awareness, every brush of his shirt sending frissons of sensation into her flesh where they multiplied and fanned out through her body, so that every part of her was acutely aware of his proximity and his every tiny touch, his every passing glance. Every part of her seemed exquisitely poised, balanced on a knife-edge, as if waiting for something to happen.

Wanting it to happen.

She drew in air that seemed charged with life, shimmering inside her as the truth of her physical wanting hit home.

He'd told her it that he wouldn't press her, that it would be her decision if they made love. Now more than ever she knew that that was what she wanted. Yet it was a different need that drove her now, compared to that she'd felt at the Gala.

There she'd been swept completely away by his sheer impact, by the physical magnetism he exuded. There she'd forgotten about the risk she was taking and the revelation that would have him recoiling in revulsion. Because his power had plugged a direct line into her needs, making her forget about everything else but wanting him and being wanted by him, reeling her in like a fish on a hook.

But tonight was different. *He* was different. He'd

talked about his family's business and his role as director, and how it gave him the involvement he wanted and the freedom to pursue his own interests. And he'd listened to her and made her feel that there was more to whatever there was between them than sheer lust. The desire was still there between them, tangible and brooding and waiting, only now it was overlaid by a sense of the man.

And the bottom line was that she liked what she saw.

From politics to the differences between countries, they'd discussed a broad range of topics—even arguing amicably over gridiron versus Australian Rules Football, and laughing when they couldn't agree about which code made the most sense. And then he'd listened when she'd told him about her family. And apart from one fearful moment, when he'd almost gone rigid with white-hot anger—what had she said to cause that?—he'd been so understanding.

Had he meant it when he'd told her that she now had him? His words had been like a balm to her soul. They'd touched her deep down, in a place where loss and pain were much more frequent visitors. She could trust him, this man. Even though she knew so little about him really, even though they'd met but on two occasions, she felt the invisible bonds between them. She could sense it.

It was rare to feel someone getting under her guard. So far only Grace had made it into her inner circle, and Grace was a hard act to follow. But the more she knew of Loukas, the more she knew that he too was special.

She could trust him with her secret. If he liked her,

as it seemed that he did, then maybe he could accept her the way she was. Maybe Grace was wrong. Maybe Loukas was special enough that it wouldn't matter to him.

She leaned her head into his shoulder as they walked and he looked down, smiling, before wrapping his arm around her and tucking her in close.

She breathed in his magic man-scent, feeling it warm her spirits like a drug. And somewhere in her mind it occurred to her that this must be exactly what it felt like to fall in love.

Fall in love?

Her steps should have faltered on the boardwalk, her breath should have caught. And yet amazingly the concept didn't scare her half as much as she thought it should. It seemed so natural, the way she was feeling, that she couldn't be scared. And, even more than natural, the idea of falling in love with Loukas seemed so inevitable.

But love didn't develop so quickly—did it? She wished she knew more. Her experience with boys and men was painfully limited, painfully inadequate. But maybe this was how it started—with an attraction, with a desire to get to know more about him.

She hugged these new sensations and her musings to herself like a precious gift as they walked along the park lining the shore to his car. It might be crazy, it might be irrational, but her heart told her that maybe she was right—that maybe Loukas was right for her.

They stopped at the car and he dropped his arm from her shoulders momentarily while he turned her towards him. He looked down at her, his eyes darker then ever away from the pier lighting.

'Thank you,' she said, her voice unusually husky. 'I enjoyed dinner—very much.'

One side of his mouth turned up. 'It's me who should be thanking you. I'm glad you agreed to come out with me.'

'One million dollars for the foundation was a powerful incentive,' she admitted with a laugh, acknowledging to herself that even without the money the evening had been more than a success as far as she was concerned.

'I hope that wasn't the only attraction,' he said, and he tilted his head fractionally so that a glimmer of light from the closest streetlamp skated over his dark eyes and disappeared under their lids as his mouth descended over hers.

Her next intake of air was full of him—his scent, his taste, the very feel of him pressed against her. He tasted of the richness of coffee and the wildness of tequila, of strength and barely contained passion, and of a need echoing hers.

His hands maintained the gentle pressure on her shoulders, anchoring her to him, but with his mouth weaving magic against hers she wasn't going anywhere. Her lips opened under his and he accepted her invitation readily, his tongue seeking entry, fusing them closer and closer together.

Her body responded in the only way it could— openly—welcoming his kiss as drought-stricken land welcomed the rain. His kiss gave her heat and life. His kiss rocked her soul. And his kiss promised so much more. She felt her breasts firm and peak, she felt her bones melt, and she knew she was lost.

'I should take you home,' he said, his slight stubble

grazing hers, his breathing sounding surprisingly ragged and edgy before his mouth found hers once more.

Boldness shaped her response. Boldness and a power driven by her need and the knowledge that it was reciprocated.

She edged her face to one side. 'Don't we have some unfinished business to take care of first?'

'You'll have your cheque first thing in the morning. I'll take care of it personally.'

She felt rather than saw the hardening of his features, the grim line of his mouth, and knew he'd misunderstood. But she refused to take offence—not when the last thing she wanted to do was start an argument between them. Not when she had a completely different purpose in mind.

She raised an arm and drew the tips of the fingers of one hand down the side of his face, circling the outer line of his ear. He swallowed then, and she followed the movement with her fingers, down the strong column of his neck, right to where it disappeared into the fine cotton of his shirt.

He looked at her quizzically, his eyes narrowing as the flat of her hand continued to stroke purposefully over his chest, resting provocatively, teasingly, over the firm nub of one nipple.

'I have a confession to make,' she said, hoping to God that now she'd finally plucked up the courage to say what she wanted she wasn't about to make a total fool of herself.

'When I referred to "unfinished business", I wasn't talking about the money.'

CHAPTER FIVE

As CONFESSIONS went it hadn't been particularly guilt-laden, but that didn't seem to worry Loukas in the least. Quite the contrary. His eyes had blazed with passion and heat in response to her words, and within half an hour he was sliding open and ushering her through the doors that led onto the balcony of his Malibu Beach house.

They stood side by side on the timber deck, staring out over the dark ocean and watching the frosted edge of the sea swoosh rhythmically in and out along the shore. The gentle summer night breeze tugged at the ends of her hair and she relished the tang of the salty sea air and tried to relax.

But she'd had thirty minutes in his car to anticipate what was to come. Thirty minutes to congratulate herself for finally being brave enough to travel a road she'd been too scared to travel in years.

Thirty minutes to panic.

What if she'd been wrong and he wasn't the man she was so desperate for him to be? And what if Grace's cold, hard words had been right? She'd never forgive herself if he changed his mind about making the donation because of what she was underneath her clothes.

Her heartbeat jumped up a gear. Suddenly this wasn't just about her own feelings. She couldn't let him know about the marks on her skin—not if it imperilled the foundation.

He interrupted her thoughts without saying a word, bringing her shoulders around to face him as he leaned against the balustrade, running his hands down her arms, taking her hands in his.

She looked up, meeting his gaze with relief. At least for now rejection was the last thing she saw in his eyes. The low light washing out over them from the living room lamps was sufficient for her to read their brown depths, and without a doubt what they told her was that he wanted her. And even in her inexperience she could tell instinctively that his want had nothing in common with the teenage testosterone-crazed mistake called Garry that marked her first sexual encounter, or even with the intense heat that had marked her first meeting with Loukas at the Gala. This time his need was accompanied by a rich bloom of tenderness that warmed her from the inside out.

And she knew in that instant that falling in love with this man wasn't just a danger. It was a fact. And if he rejected her now for any reason...

She trembled as the fear rippled through her. This time there was more at stake than merely trampling on her self-worth. There was even more at stake than the financial security of the foundation. This time it could be her heart that was battered.

'Are you cold?' he asked.

She shook her head, surprised that he'd so quickly picked up on her feelings of discomfiture. 'No, it's not that.'

'Then what...?'

She could feel the heat rising in her face as she struggled to answer, already regretting her quick denial. It would have been easier to agree that she *was* cold. How could she possibly admit that she was afraid without telling him everything?

She could so easily imagine the type of women he was used to dating. They would be sophisticated and poised, with the confidence that came from being surrounded from birth with money and opportunity—hardly the type to feel uncertain about their place in the world. That was what he was probably expecting with her. As a successful doctor, with a growing and successful clientele, that was exactly how she should be—how she *would* be, if it weren't for the scars.

He was looking down at her, waiting, expecting her to say something. And she knew she had to find some words to try to explain something of what she was feeling.

'I warn you now, I'm not very good at this,' she admitted at last, with a weak smile forced out briefly around gritted teeth. 'I'm actually—a bit nervous.'

His eyes narrowed and he angled his head closer to his shoulder, almost as if weighing up her words. What was he thinking? She held her breath, wondering what it meant for their budding relationship if even that tiny admission was making him reconsider his plans for the night.

'Are you telling me that you're a virgin?'

She blinked, momentarily taken aback that she'd so totally misinterpreted his look. But wasn't that exactly how she'd sounded? Like some timorous virgin?

'Heavens, no!' she protested. Garry had well and truly taken care of that, before discovering her secret and throwing her out of the car. Then, because she thought she'd made it sound as if there was something wrong with being a virgin, and because losing her virginity wasn't something she was particularly proud of given the inglorious circumstances, she dropped her head and added, 'Well, just no, really.'

His fingers found her chin, encouraging her with gentle pressure to lift her gaze once more to his. Her lungs clamped down, the gentle lap of the waves against the shore drowned out by the drumbeat of her pulse as she searched his face. His eyes looked almost doubtful.

He must be having second thoughts this time. Her inexperience was bound to be a turn-off for a man like Loukas. He'd be used to partners who could give as good as they got—partners who could provide pleasure even as they were accepting it. There hadn't been too much of that in her experience. Quick sex in the back seat of a car didn't leave too much time for covering much more than the basic mechanics.

He moved his hand then, so that her chin rested against his palm and his long fingers cupped her cheek. 'How about we take things slowly, then?'

She could have kissed him then and there—if only because at least now she could breathe again. As it was, she didn't need to go to the effort, because his lips were upon hers, slanting in a series of passes that had her wanting to catch his mouth and hold it prisoner against hers for ever.

His hand slipped behind her head, his fingers tangling in her hair and unwinding the casual knot she'd tied it into so that the length of it tumbled over her shoulders. He growled and pulled her closer, and yet his touch was still tender, unhurried, as he continued his exploration of her back, skimming the fabric of her silk blouse with a touch that was gentle and yet devastating in impact. His hands swooped lower, capturing her behind, and his arms moulded to the shape of her, so she could feel him all around her, feel his heat feeding into her, feel him pressing her closer against his hardness. And all the while he used his lips to woo her.

It would be all right.

His message was relayed to her in his kiss, in the touch of his mouth to her throat, and in the warm, mellifluous world he'd transported her to.

There was no panic, there was no hurried rush, there was no frantic desperation in his movements. There was only a languid inevitability about his exploration of her mouth and her body.

She steeled herself for his first contact with her breast, knowing it would come, forcing herself in the warm blanket of his attentions not to be scared, not to panic. It didn't have to be like before.

They could make love.

He didn't have to know.

He didn't have to see.

And then his large hands were there, scooping under the curve of her breasts, leaving her breathless as ecstasy melded with fear. His thumbs flicked over her nipples and she felt them harden under his touch as sensation drove exquisitely downwards. His mouth at her throat, she tried to maintain her breathing. She tried to take control over the unfamiliar feelings of some tissues firming, others plumping and slickening. But she had no power to haul herself back—not when he dropped to his knees and placed his mouth over one breast.

She shuddered in his arms. Even though the silk of her blouse and the layer of satin beneath, the tropical heat of his mouth made her gasp and arch her back.

Her hands clung to his head, losing their fingers in his thick dark waves as his teeth tugged on her nipple and his hands dipped to the backs of her knees.

The shock of his hands against the bare skin of her legs, circling upwards, threatened to melt her bones. She swayed, clinging to Loukas with one arm for support, reaching out to find the balustrade with the other, knowing even in the fog of her desire that she needed to hang on to something more grounded if she wasn't to topple right over.

He seemed to sense their precarious position, his hands ceasing their ascent of her thighs as he removed his mouth from her breast, trailing kisses up her throat until she was in his arms again and she could let go her hold on the balustrade with Loukas to anchor her.

'You're so beautiful,' he said, before his mouth descended on hers again.

It was meant as a compliment, but it hit her like an accusation. She wasn't beautiful. He wouldn't say that if he knew.

And he didn't know because she wasn't being honest with him. If she were, she would tell him beforehand—and just maybe he'd understand. Maybe he wouldn't think she was a freak. Maybe it wouldn't change anything.

But, then again, maybe it would.

The look on Garry's face came back—the revulsion, the contorted features of his face, as he realised what he'd just had sex with, when he realised she wasn't what he'd expected. And all the good feeling about the success of her latest treatment, all the joy at finally being able to lift up her head in Yarrabee, the excitement of even finding a boy willing to be her partner for the senior dance—all of it had evaporated in one bitter moment.

She'd realised in that instant, and confirmed in the tears she'd shed into her pillow that night, that she would never be like other women.

She knew she should tell Loukas. She should warn him. But she couldn't. At least not until afterwards when, no matter what his reaction, at least she would have experienced the magic of one time with him. Was it wrong to want that? Was it wrong to just want one magical time?

Because there was no doubt it would be a world away from what she'd experienced that one fractured summer back in Yarrabee.

So she didn't say a word. She just kissed him back with all the feelings welling up inside her that came so naturally now, with all the sensations that he'd unleashed within her. And before she knew it he'd scooped her up into his arms and, still kissing her, carried her inside the house.

There'd never been a moment she'd felt so alive. Her senses were buzzing with so many different emotions, so many different needs, and all of them were directly sparked by one man and directed to one outcome.

She felt herself being lowered onto a bed, and he knelt down almost reverentially alongside her, his body a dark silhouette against the dull yellow glow from the lamps filtering in from the hallway.

'I've wanted to make love to you since the moment I first saw you,' he whispered, his voice husky and thick.

'I know,' she said, because she knew it was the truth. 'I've felt it too.'

He reached a hand over to a side-table and she caught his intent.

'No!' She caught his arm with her hand, stopping him before he hit the switch. And then, in case he read too much into the urgency in her voice, she whispered, 'Please?'

'I understand,' he said, moving away from the lamp. 'We'll take it slowly.'

And he did. Take her slowly. Bit by bit, achingly slowly, he peeled the clothes from them both, running his hands over her skin as each garment came off, setting her flesh alight. And in the darkness she knew she was safe. In the darkness she knew she could give herself up to the pleasure she was feeling, the pleasure he was giving her.

And she had never experienced such pleasure! Wherever his hands went his hot mouth followed closely behind. Such simple gestures—the liquid sweep of lips against skin, the hypnotic swirl of tongue against flesh, the gentle rasp of teeth—such simple movements, and yet so arousing, so breathtakingly erotic.

Lost in awe and wonder, and given up to sensations far out of her experience, she let his mouth go wherever he wanted. She let his lips dance around her navel, let him flick the tip of his tongue inside, tickling and exploring and foreshadowing the act that was to come. She let him do whatever he wanted because of how he made her feel, so that when his mouth descended over the peak of her scarred breast she reacted with little more than a panicked hitch to her breath—and even that soon evaporated in the heat of a scorching bliss the likes of which she'd never known.

But when he insinuated a knee between her legs and dipped his head lower she knew she wasn't just going beyond her experience, he was taking her beyond reason. Her back arched as he found her core, his tongue making lazy circles around her most sensitive flesh, lapping at her, teasing her entrance, so that she called out for him to end the torture, to end the search for culmination.

Her hands curled tightly into the bedclothes, her shoulders twisted as she wriggled to escape, but his arms held tight on her thighs, anchoring her to him so that she had no hope but to ride the wild waves that were building inside her—no hope but to go with them, higher and higher. Until his mouth gave one final teasing suckle to her tender flesh and the waves crashed down, spilling her over the edge, tossing her like balsa into the foaming wash of her passion.

He clung to her as the final waves moved through her, turning to ripples and disappearing like the tide slipping out, and then he moved to her side, pulling her in close, hugging her to him as she gasped her way back to something approximating normality.

But she knew she would never be normal again. He'd shattered every preconceived notion she'd had about sex in one cataclysmic act. She'd always thought it should be good, known it ought to be good, but never had she realised how good it could be. And still she hadn't felt the power of him inside her. How much better would *that* be?

She nuzzled into his shoulder, already tingling at the prospect, relishing the musky scent of him and the feel of his body, still fully charged, wrapped around hers. His hands were skimming the side of her body from shoulder to mid-thigh and back again, movements that escalated her desire all over again.

'I thought you said you were going to take things slowly,' she whispered.

He laughed, a low, deep rumble that she felt to her toes. 'One thing at a time,' he answered, rolling her once more onto her back, his mouth coming down hard on hers.

This time she was more aware. This time she was able to hold him, to explore the skinscape of his broad shoulders and the well-defined surface of his back, tapering as if sculpted into his firm waist before rising again into the taut swell of his buttocks.

He groaned as her hands pressed down on him, her thumbs finding the sweat-slickened hollows of his lower back, her fingers curling into his flesh as she felt the press of his erection, proof of his own unanswered need, hard against her.

And in that moment she understood how much he'd given her already. He hadn't just slaked his need on her in an instant—as he could have done, as she would have let him. He hadn't just taken what he could have. Instead he'd bestowed pleasure upon her first. He'd given her the chance to find her own paradise without greedily seeking his own.

Whatever came after this, whatever followed— whether it was his censure or his pity—she would never regret this night. Whatever happened, however foolhardy her love proved to be, she would always love him for what he had just given her.

He rolled away for a moment, retrieved something from the bedside table that quickly made good sense, and then he was back, lifting himself higher over her, and she knew with an innate woman sense what he wanted. Because it was what she wanted too. And then he was between her thighs, poised, waiting.

The electric charge of first contact ripped a gasp from her throat that had nothing to do with pain and everything to do with exquisitely intense sensation. Every muscle inside her clamped down, trying to capture him, to draw him inside.

He growled, low and rough, as he answered her with more of him, then eased back before stretching her further.

It was torture.

It was bliss.

She tilted her hips, welcoming his length, encouraging him further, and when she gasped again it was in wonder at his sheer size, stretching her limits, filling her so completely that their bodies met, their union complete.

For a moment he stilled, a moment that shone in time with brilliant clarity, as if she was teetering on the edge. And if she thought that what he'd done before had changed her life, then what he was doing now was something so profound and meaningful that she felt her entire world changing. Then he moved, slowly, teasingly withdrawing, and she felt air rush into her lungs as if to fill the void.

Then he lunged, filling her completely once more, leaving no space for anything but him. Slowly at first he built the rhythm, taking her with him as he moved inside her, as he built the pace. And she went with him, matching him, taking his lead, feeling the pressure building inexorably inside her yet again, the urgency, the desperate race for completion.

Until his surging thrusts sent her spinning for a second time, light and weightless, as the wave of shimmering ecstasy lifted her out of herself to a place where nothing was important, nothing mattered, other than her blissful acceptance of his own shuddering, pumping release.

They lay together, their limbs entwined, their breathing raggedly steadying, bodies slick and spent.

Loukas stared blankly up towards the darkened ceiling, mentally congratulating himself on his unexpected progress. She'd fallen in with his plans much more quickly than he'd anticipated. How much longer should he wait before he could start asking her questions?

He turned his head to where he could just make out her profile in the darkened room, just see the line of her closed eyes, her slightly parted lips, as she replenished her oxygen-depleted lungs. New questions sprang to mind—new questions that had nothing to do with the reason why she was here.

What was she hiding?

How could someone who looked like her be so inexperienced? Why would she be so shy? None of it made sense.

He'd scarcely believed her claim on the deck to be nervous, and yet she *was* an ingénue, and her performance had proved her near-innocence. She hadn't lied to him—she'd been no virgin—though she had been deliciously tight and so responsive. She'd accepted his caresses with genuine enthusiasm, and yet made no attempt to reciprocate or take control. She'd made no attempt to explore his body beyond his chest and back. She'd made no attempt take him in her hand.

His body hummed at the thought, already anticipating that act. He'd like to feel her soft fingers curl around him, maybe even... He felt a sudden rush of blood at the prospect. No, she might not be a virgin but she was the next best thing. It would be more than gratifying to teach her more, to have her learn more of what he liked.

And why shouldn't he make the most of this opportunity? It had been a long time since he'd been interested in a woman.

It had been a long time since Zoë.

His breathing stilled, before softly expelling the air in his lungs on a sigh as he curled one hand behind his head. Four years it would be, come December. Four years since her vivacious green eyes had danced for him, and he'd wound her long dark hair around his hands and tugged her laughing mouth closer to his.

But then, it was probably longer still than that. It might be coming up to four years since she'd died, but they'd not made love for months before her death. He'd accepted her claims of illness or inconvenience for far too long, not realising that under her clothes her five-foot-ten-inch frame had been reduced to little more than a walking skeleton. And yet still she'd complained of being fat, exercising herself until she'd collapsed.

She'd never been fat, even when they'd first met, and he'd had no inkling of the insecurities lurking below her glamorous exterior. But even before she'd become so ill, so obsessed with the body beautiful and how cosmetic surgery could lend a hand, he'd never found on her the lush curves he'd enjoyed so much tonight.

He expelled a burst of air, guilt seeping into his consciousness. No, it had been too long if he was starting to compare the likes of this woman with Zoë.

Zoë didn't deserve it.

Still, that needn't stop him from pursuing his plan. He had the time now. The latest from his father said that Olympia was leaving on a shopping trip to Paris in the morning, meaning she was safe from Della-Bosca's witchcraft for a few days at least.

Which gave him the perfect opportunity to take his time with Jade.

He'd get the information he wanted. There was no doubt of that. Already he could sense her attitude warming to him, her once prickly defences coming down. A few more days of this and she would be his to control. She'd tell him everything he wanted to know and more. She wouldn't stand a chance.

But first he'd make the most of her refreshingly innocent body. He'd teach her how to pleasure a man. He'd teach her how to pleasure *him*. And then he'd take as much of her as he had time for.

He turned fully to her, running his hand along her sensual side-on curves and stirring her provocatively back into wakefulness.

There was no time like the present to begin.

CHAPTER SIX

'LOUKAS? It's Con.' His father's strident tones boomed down the landline. 'Olympia is back in the States.'

Loukas reeled and checked the chronometer on his watch. *Not already!* 'Are you certain?'

'I told you she was only going for three to four days! She called her mother today when she got back. Stella dropped that she's going in for some "home improvements" this week. So, what have you found out?'

'I'm…working on it,' Loukas managed, trying to work out where in God's name three days had gone.

'What? I thought you had that girl eating out of your hand? What the hell have you been doing?'

Loukas took a desperate gasp for oxygen. *Eating out of his hand.* He might have used those exact words himself the last time he'd called his father, but eating out of his hand wasn't the direction his thoughts had been going in just lately. Not the way his student had been so skilfully progressing. 'It's— more complicated than I thought.'

'No way!'

'Listen, Con, about Jade—she's not what we assumed. It's taking more time to get what I want.'

'There is no more time! You know what those paparazzi are like. I'm trying to run on a family ticket and I haven't got time right now to come over and sort Olympia out. The papers will make a meal out of me if they snap her coming out of a place like that. So you need to find her first. You have to find out when she's scheduled for surgery and you have to keep her out of there.'

'I know that,' he said. 'I'm trying to.'

'Then try harder. Have you tried calling her lately?'

'You know she won't take my calls—not after what happened before. Chasing her halfway across the country to stop her from making the mistake of her life and marrying Kurt sure hasn't helped me out in the big brother stakes. She's not likely to talk to me any time soon, Con.'

'Then use that woman of yours more effectively. She knows something. If she's in with Della-Bosca then she has to. Find out what it is and stop her.'

Loukas raked his fingers through his hair as he looked skyward. Yeah, what his father said all made sense, but... Just lately he'd been beginning to think he'd made a mistake. For all the things he'd thought so fake about Jade, she seemed so real in his arms. And she felt damned real in his bed.

'Loukas!'

'I'm here.'

'This is more important than ever. You can't let Olympia get dragged through the papers. Not now. It's crucial you stop her.'

'I know. I'll sort it out for her. She's my sister, after all. I'm not going to let anything happen to her.'

'She's not your sister.'

'Well, half-sister, then. It's the same thing isn't it? She's family.'

'Listen to me, Loukas. Very carefully. She's *not* your sister. Not by blood, at any rate.'

The silence hung between them, a dank and heavy curtain that smothered conversation for several seconds.

'What are you saying? I thought that was why you married Stella—because she was having your baby.'

'That's what I thought too. And, even though her colouring was all wrong, I was too besotted with your stepmother back then to think anything of the baby's blonde hair. All I cared about was that ten years after your mother had died I'd been lucky enough to find another beautiful wife and father another child. It never occurred to me then that Olympia might not be mine.'

'So she's not my sister—at all?' No wonder they'd never connected—on any level. It wasn't just half a generation and attitudes that separated them, it was their parentage as well.

'Unless your father was a Scandinavian prince— no.' He hesitated. 'Which is why nobody wants this getting out to the press. Not a sniff. Everything has to stay locked down—until after the primaries at least.'

'How long have you known?' Loukas asked.

He could hear his father's irritated exhalation all those miles away. The older man was still angry about it. 'It started to bug me when she was growing up— let's face it, she hardly looked like a Demakis! But it was only about eight months ago that Stella finally confirmed it—that I didn't father Olympia.'

'Eight months ago?' echoed Loukas, nodding as another piece of the puzzle slotted into place. 'Just before she suddenly took off with the brat-pack and married Kurt.'

'Well, I sure as hell didn't tell her!' his father said. 'It was Stella. She thought she had a right to know.'

It all made sense to Loukas. No wonder she'd gone so far off the rails. She'd always fought against all things Demakis—news like that would have been the last straw. And he could see why his father didn't want the press involved. If the scandal sheets got hold of a story like this before the elections they'd have a field day.

'Can't Stella help you get through to her now?'

'Pia won't listen to her—not now she's got that bum Kurt telling her what to do. She only calls her mother up now to irritate the hell out of her. She says her mother betrayed her, should never have married me. Now she feels vindicated for hating me all these years, and it's payback time for Stella.' He hauled in a long burst of air.

'But Olympia has to be stopped, and you're the only one who can reach her. Nobody knows better than you what this Della-Bosca woman is capable of. You have to get her out of there, Loukas, no matter what it takes!'

Tonight was the night. For three days now she'd lived a life of bliss, being whisked away by Loukas to the Malibu Beach house and made love to late into the night. Life had never been so good. Life had never been so happy.

Only guilt threatened to cloud her joy—the guilt that she hadn't been honest with him.

Jade finished writing up the notes from her last pa-

tient for the day and closed down her computer.
Loukas would be collecting her soon, and already her
blood fizzed in anticipation. But this time more than
ever it was anticipation tinged with foreboding.

She entered the *en suite* bathroom adjoining her
office to freshen up. Every day she'd sworn that this
night would be the one—that she'd reveal her secret
tonight, that she would leave the light on and take off
her clothes and let him discover the truth.

And every night her resolve to tell Loukas had been
blown away by the sheer force of their lovemaking
and the knowledge that things would have to change
once he knew.

Her face stared back at her in the mirror. What
would it be like for him to see her scars for the first
time? Would he think them as bad as she anticipated
or worse? How would he react? In horror? In revulsion? Or would it just turn him off completely? There
weren't a lot of options, and none of them were good.
He could hardly react with joy.

On a sudden whim she lifted the hem of her knitted
top and pulled it over her head before she could
change her mind. Her satin and lace bra followed. She
needed to prepare herself for what was to come. She
needed to be able to face what she expected him to.

She opened her eyes and looked into the mirror.
First at her eyes—a little bewildered, a lot afraid—
then at her mussed hair, and finally to the red mottled
stain that started on one side of her ribcage and crept
up like a red wine stain on a white tablecloth, the
edges crazily uneven, to devour most of her left
breast.

She squeezed her eyes shut. The contrast with her

untanned white skin only accentuated the scars. And if she found it ugly...

But it couldn't be put off any longer. No more covering up with robes, with lace teddies and negligees. No more hiding from the light, no more deception. If she couldn't trust Loukas now, after what they'd shared, then she was never going to be able to trust him.

She summoned all the strength she had as she replaced her clothes, smoothing her hair before heading for the exit.

Tonight was the night!

She was waiting for him outside the clinic, just as they'd arranged, and one sight of her was enough to quicken his pulse in anticipation of what the night would bring. She'd been such a good student, eager and quick to learn, turning from an innocent into a she-devil in less time than he would have imagined possible even under his skilful tutelage.

And yet he hadn't managed to transform her completely. She was a strange mix—so sexy with her new knowledge one minute, and yet still so shy and innocent the next. She continued to plead to make love in the dark, as he hungered to see her body stripped of the shadows she preferred to adorn herself with.

But time had run out. He gritted his teeth as he remembered his father's call. Olympia was back, and about to book herself into the clinic at any time. Which meant there was no more time for instruction of his protégée—no more time to break down her last remaining barriers.

And that annoyed him intensely.

How could time have slipped away so quickly? He wasn't finished with her yet—not by a long way. He hadn't had enough of her lush curves, her responsive body, the incredible feeling of her shattering in his arms as he pumped into her.

His teeth clenched as he pulled into the kerb alongside her, noticing the way the breeze sculpted the soft fabric of her skirt around the sensational legs beneath. Legs that climbed all the way up to a place where he'd found paradise for the last three nights. A place that would be available to him only in his memories once she discovered his real purpose.

He rammed the heel of his hand against the steering wheel.

Damn his father!

Damn his sister and her useless husband!

And damn Della-Bosca and the industry that fed like parasites off the insecure, fuelling their endless pursuit for the perfect body!

He lifted his eyes from Jade's legs long enough to notice her slight frown—too bad if she'd picked up on his mood, he was too angry to pretend everything was all right. And it didn't matter if he wasn't the perfect host tonight. He had a more important job to do.

She had to tell him whatever she knew. Whatever Della-Bosca had planned for his sister he would have to prevent. And then hopefully he would have enough evidence to put her away for life. It was time someone did.

*   *   *

'You seem tense,' she said, when finally, after a conversation-starved journey, they arrived at the house. 'Is something the matter?'

She waited while he fixed them both a drink, almost afraid to breathe, already rethinking her plans to come clean. Could it be that he was tiring of her already? Was her lack of experience and finesse a turn-off for him?

The thought almost paralysed her with a kind of grief—the last few nights had been the best in her life, and Loukas was the reason. But if he didn't want her any more…

He turned then, and what she saw almost made her recoil—because for the briefest second his face looked exactly as it had done the first time she'd seen him: harsh and unforgiving and etched with a hostility she couldn't fathom. But then in a blink of his eyes it was gone, replaced by a smile she'd become more familiar with, a smile that seemed so warm and sincere she almost reeled in confusion, wondering whether she'd imagined the transformation.

But she *had* seen that momentary flash in his eyes, the chiselled set of his chin. Underneath the façade he was angry with her—but why?

Unless he knew! Fear pooled deep down in her gut, turning the contents of her stomach to rebellion mode. She'd thought she was being careful enough, but maybe he'd discovered her secret himself. Maybe he was furious with her for not telling him, for deceiving him—just like Garry had been.

It was history repeating itself. Here was another man she'd hidden the truth from. Another man deceived. Why the hell hadn't she learned something from her first appalling experience? Why the hell had she waited to tell Loukas?

Fool, she thought, as he left the drinks on the bar and closed the distance between them empty-handed. Her stomach churned, her feet seemingly cemented to the floor when all she really wanted to do was flee. Of course she'd waited! Because she'd known exactly what would happen once she told him—she wouldn't see him for dust. And she would have missed out on three incredible nights, the scorching memories of which were going to keep her warm at night long after he was gone.

Was that what he was building up to now? Was this the end?

She swallowed as he came to a standstill in front of her, the action forcing up her chin defiantly. 'Have I done something wrong?' She'd dredged confidence from somewhere. Her words sounded far braver than she felt. But she had to know where she stood. Her mind was already working on her defence. *I was going to tell you! Now! Tonight!*

He said nothing, the wine glasses on the bar forgotten, the look on his face confusing her—too many tangled emotions to make sense of, too much to understand. Then a muscle in his jaw spasmed, lifting the corner of his mouth, and somehow the layers seemed to slide from his features, the anger, the resentment dissolving away, so that all that was left was undisguised and all the more potent. Raw desire—need—there was no misinterpreting his message now.

'I'm not actually all that thirsty any more,' he said, his breath brushing lightly across her cheek, setting her skin to prickling awareness all the way down to her toes. 'How about you?'

His eyes riveted her to the spot. She could no sooner take her eyes from his than walk to the moon. She gave a single barely-there shake of her head. 'No,' she said.

He smiled then, and curved his arms around her neck, the pads of his fingers still cool from the wine glasses while the reaction they triggered was anything but. His thumbs stroked her earlobes, tugging gently on her gold hoops. Her eyelids fluttered closed. There was something wonderfully sexy about the way he did that, something strangely hypnotic—his eyes locked on hers, his fingers tugging, insistent, on her soft flesh.

Then his mouth dipped to hers, and it was the turn of his mouth to catch her bottom lip, securing the plump flesh between his teeth before releasing it. Again and again he repeated the tender gesture, as sweetly as if he were playing an instrument, while she stood entranced, eyes closed, the rhythm of his gentle movements building on the need mounting, coiling inside.

Only when he released her lip one final time did she open her eyes. He sighed then, almost as if he was reluctantly giving himself over to something he didn't quite understand, but there was no time to ponder his expression once he uttered his next words.

'Then come to bed.'

And, just like his caresses, his lovemaking was slow and languid, his movements designed to extract every last drop of pleasure from the act. His hands explored her skin, rounding over her curves, dipping into her hollows, taking his time as if he was reading her through his fingertips. And all the while his mouth worshipped her, tasting her, laving her.

Slow, exquisite torture. The pace suited her mood, matched her needs. And gave her the time to drink in his body, to memorise the lines of his sculpted torso. Because she would tell him tonight—in the lush afterglow of sex, when the memory of their lovemaking might mellow his response. And then finally there would be no lies between them, no deception.

But that would be later. Right now she accepted each tender kiss, each gentle caress, mentally documenting them along with every taste, every different texture of his skin, storing them away as if they might be her last opportunity.

And even when they finally came together—their bodies so slick as if oiled, their breathing coming fast—even then he controlled the pace, driving into her purposefully, lending his entire length to her, then resting subtly before withdrawing, achingly slowly, tormenting her, driving her crazy before thrusting into her again. And in this way, slowly, steadily, inexorably, she felt it building, an overwhelming force that lifted her higher and higher as he continued his relentless drive into her until there was nowhere left to go, nowhere left to climb.

She sensed his body still, accepted one more surging thrust, and with a cry she came apart, clutching at the bedclothes, clutching for him, clutching to keep a hold on a universe that was coming to pieces all around her. He shuddered into her, prolonging her release, sending her spinning even further out of control with his own pulsing energy to a place beyond reason, beyond experience.

She lay in his arms gasping for air as the last waves rocked through her, gradually subsiding. His heartbeat was like a drum, rock steady, pulling her back to normality. It had never been this good. It had never felt that powerful. And there was no question that she'd been wrong.

It wasn't over between them. No way could you make love like that with a person who meant nothing to you. Even with her limited experience of relationships, that much at least seemed obvious. Loukas must feel something for her. Even if it in no way matched the heart-swelling surge of this new love she felt for him, *he had to feel something*.

And that knowledge gave her courage. She would tell him. This didn't have to be a repeat of that night in Yarrabee. Garry had never cared about her. Both of them had wanted different things that night. She'd wanted to finally know what it was like to have a boy interested in you—a boy who thought you were pretty enough to take out and make feel special. But all Garry had wanted was a quick lay.

She shoved the bitter memories back to the past where they belonged. Loukas wouldn't react the same way—couldn't react the same way—not after what they'd shared together. And if he did? Her heart rate jerked up a notch. When he discovered she was imperfect, that she was scarred, that she was not the woman he'd thought her to be, would he really accept her then?

She swallowed back her fears. It made no difference now. The time had come.

'Loukas?' she murmured, unable to resist the temptation of running her fingers over his muscular chest, through the wiry spring of the dark hairs, around the firm nub of his nipple for what might well end up being the last time.

His hand snared hers, stilling her movements, holding her captive. The suddenness of his action startled her, as did the rough way he abruptly discarded her hand and twisted away, almost wrenching his arm out from underneath her.

'What is it?'

His voice sounded strangely harsh, as if he'd returned to that dark mood he'd been in earlier, and she felt her courage waver. The way he'd left her side, turning his back on her—so much for taking advantage of the warm afterglow of love. But she couldn't put it off any longer. She couldn't keep this secret for ever. And the longer she tried, the more difficult it would become, the more dangerous the possible repercussions.

'Loukas,' she repeated softly, steeling herself for the inevitable shock that would follow her revelation. 'T-turn on the light. I've got something to tell you.'

CHAPTER SEVEN

HE ROSE from the bed, bile burning in the back of his throat, the passions of the last half-hour obliterated in the knowledge that he had to act soon if he had any chance of saving his sister.

'I hope so,' he tossed in reply, without turning. 'It's time someone shed some light on things around here.' He threw her robe across to the bed automatically, as he'd learned to do the last few nights, acceding to the bizarre code of embarrassment she lived by.

Without looking back he zipped himself into a pair of jeans, and then he stood at the window, watching the reflection from the moon light a path across the water.

He'd known it would come to this since the first moment they'd met. There was no way for them ever to be more than enemies—not in the long run—not with what he had to do. And now, after what his father had told him, now there was no way around it. So why was he hesitating? Why now was he finding it so difficult to do that about which he had no choice?

Because you're going to hurt her.

He pushed the thought back to where it had sprung from. That shouldn't be a consideration—it was inevitable that she would be upset, but it had never factored into the equation before. So why now?

'Loukas?'

He gazed out over the bay, watching the water

shimmer under the path of the moonlight while everywhere beyond was black. Zoë had loved the sea. She'd once shone as brilliantly as that slash of light bisecting the water, making everyone and everything around her fade into amorphous shades of grey.

But she didn't shine any more. She would never shine again. Grace Della-Bosca and her cronies had extinguished the spark that had been Zoë, preying on her insecurities, feeding her own self-doubts, and ultimately destroying her with a drug-crazed hand.

And he'd be damned if Della-Bosca was going to get a chance to do the same to his sister!

He swung around, facing the bed and its sole occupant, both little more than dull shapes in the dark room.

'Tell me what you know about my sister, Olympia.'

Silence followed his question. He saw the outline that was Jade move to sit up, reaching for what he took to be her robe.

'I didn't even know you had a sister. You've never mentioned her.'

He laughed out loud. As if he'd have to mention it! He knew Olympia was a client. She'd told her mother she was booked in—there was no mistake. 'Surely you don't expect me to believe that?'

'You can believe what you like, but it's the truth. As far as I know I've never met your sister. What makes you think I have?'

'Come on! Is that what *she* tells you to say whenever someone starts asking difficult questions?'

'What *who* tells me to say?'

Her voice had dropped the defensive attitude and taken on a more argumentative tone. Good! Maybe he might get somewhere yet. He watched her silhouette rise from the bed, saw movement as she thrust her arms into the robe.

'Who do you think? That woman you work for. Della-Bosca.'

'You're talking about *Dr* Della-Bosca, I take it?'

She rounded the bed, snapping a switch as she reached the door, and suddenly everything moved from the shadows and was bathed in colour and light.

He looked at her, at the dishevelled hair flying untamed around her colour-tinged cheeks, her accusing eyes, the peacock-blue robe cinched tightly around her waist and her arms crossed firmly over her chest, and he realised all too soon his mistake.

So much for the softly-softly approach he'd intended! Instead he'd gone in all guns blazing, and now it was too late to pull back. Especially when all her continued denials achieved was to further fuel his anger.

'Why bother to call her a doctor at all?' he sniped. 'Witch doctor would be more appropriate!'

Her gasp told him he'd punched the air right out of her lungs, and her features were masked with shock. *Thank God.* She needed to hear the truth, even if she didn't like it. She had to face up to the kind of woman she was working for—the kind of woman she herself was no doubt becoming, if she wasn't already there. Why else would she defend her so stridently?

'What the hell is wrong with you all of a sudden?' she demanded, unfolding her arms only to plant her hands defiantly on her hips. 'Grace is doing work that's world-renowned. You know that. Who are you to criticise her? What is your problem?'

'I expected you to defend her.'

'Of course I'm going to defend her! Somebody needs to, given she's not here to defend herself. Who the hell are you to attack her this way?'

'Who am I? Just someone who knows what she's really like. Someone who has seen what that monster can do and think she can get away with it. And someone who's going to make damn sure she doesn't get a chance to destroy my sister's life!'

By the time he'd finished his outburst he was shouting, his chest heaving, one hand curled into a fist, ramming against the air with every point he made.

This was madness. Her mind reeled under the force of his tirade, the force of his hatred. But she had to stay calm—stay calm, breathe deeply, and then get the hell out of there!

'I told you before, and I'm telling you now, I don't know and have never heard of your sister.' Her voice surprised her with its even quality. *Thank God.* Someone had to keep control here. She took another lungful of air, praying that her tone would have some soothing effect on Loukas's mood. 'Come and search our database if you don't believe me. There is no Olympia Demakis on our files anywhere.'

'She's married.' He spat the words out impatiently, as if she should have known. 'Her name is Kovac now.'

'Kovac?' The cogs in her mind freewheeled before crunching to a grinding halt before a petite blonde-haired girl with massive insecurities. *Surely not.* But the first name—she could have shortened it...

'Are you telling me that *Pia* Kovac is your sister?'

'Pia.' He sniffed as his eyes lit up with a ferocious gleam. Of course. He should have known she'd erase anything from her life that reminded her of her Greek father. 'So you do know her. You've known of her all along.'

'I had no idea she was your sister. You two look nothing alike.'

That's because she's not my sister, he thought with a dose of bitterness, still getting used to the idea. Instead he said, 'Olympia is the child of my father's second wife.'

Who was obviously not of Greek descent, Jade thought, scratching to find any similarities between Loukas and Pia in either looks or personality that might have warned her the two were related. What had happened to his mother? She knew nothing about his family though she'd told him so much of her own. Why was that?

'So when is she scheduled for surgery? I will come and collect her from the clinic before it.'

Loukas's question broke into her thoughts, his assumption that he could just walk in and take control of his sister clashing violently with everything she knew about doctor-patient ethics.

'Now, hang on! I can't discuss that with you. Matters between a patient and her doctor are confidential.'

'But you will talk to her about this surgery. Tell her not to go ahead!'

'I've already spoken to her, and she wants to go ahead with the procedures.' She didn't have to tell him that she'd already tried to talk the girl out of the breast augmentation operation. Jade wasn't comfortable with the extent of the surgery, or the way that Grace seemed almost too eager to accede to her requests. 'And while I can advise her, ultimately it's Pia's choice—not mine, and most definitely not yours. Like it or not, you just have to respect that.'

'You can't let her do this. You have to stop her!'

She shook her head. 'I don't see how I can stop her. I don't understand why I should even try.'

'She will not be operated on by that woman! I won't allow it.'

'Then why don't *you* tell her that? She's *your* sister after all. Why don't you just go and stop her yourself?'

He spun around and faced the window, looking out to sea. He was like a storm cloud in the otherwise clear night sky. He was crashing waves and dangerous reefs and she'd been well and truly shipwrecked. And she'd all but steered a course for those rocks herself, ensuring she'd be smashed to smithereens.

But maybe she wasn't his only victim. Maybe she wasn't all he'd wrecked.

'I get it now,' she said to the strong lines of his back. 'You two don't get along.'

'She's not talking to me at the moment. That's all.'

'So little sister doesn't like being bossed around and bullied by big brother?'

'It's not like that,' he said, facing her. 'I was trying to stop her doing something stupid. I tried to stop her marrying that celebrity disaster, but she wouldn't listen to me—and now she's stuck with him.'

'So it is like that! I can believe it. Well, I've got news for you. I don't like being pushed around either! Whatever this communication problem you have with your sister, *you* work it out. Don't expect me to do your dirty work.'

She turned and let her eyes scour the floor, looking to pick up her scattered clothes. His hand closed around her arm like an iron manacle.

'I won't have her so much as touched by that woman!'

She wrenched back on her arm, but it was stuck firm in his grip. 'You're mad,' she sneered through bared teeth. 'I don't understand what your problem is with plastic surgery in general or with Grace in particular, but you're wrong—you're way off base.'

'Am I? So the drug-taking, her operating stoned, the scarring she's caused—the deaths!—all of that is off base too?'

'*What?*'

'You can't pretend you don't know. You can't pretend you haven't heard the stories—the botched surgeries, the hushed-up case histories.'

'None of what you're saying is true—none of it.'

'Forget it, Jade. You don't have to defend her now. I'm giving you the chance to come clean and tell the real story. Get it off your conscience.'

'Okay. I *do* know the real story. I work with the woman. I live with her! And what I know is that you shouldn't believe every piece of dirt you hear about a person. So you've heard rumours—they're nothing more. How do you think Grace could keep operating if any of those stories were true?'

'*No!*' He let go his grip on her arm and slammed his open palm down on the dressing table. 'You don't get out of this with that *rumour* crap. I *know* those stories are real. I *know* what she's like—what she's done.'

'And *how* do you know? What the hell is she supposed to have done that could be so damning? And don't give me any more rumours or hearsay—I want to hear what you think you know. Just what has Grace done that is so damned bad?'

He loomed over her, looking larger and more dominating right now than she'd ever seen him. She saw the spark of fire in his eyes, saw his lips peel back from his teeth. He reminded her of a wild animal going in for the strike—and for the first time tonight she felt truly afraid.

'You want to hear what she did? You really want to know? Then listen to this—because it's no rumour. Your whiter-than-snow doctor murdered my fiancée.'

The room spun and whirled—or was it just her mind, overcome with Loukas's crazy claims? She had to get away—he was too close, too imposing. The way his eyes flashed with something that looked like triumph—it had to be a form of madness, whatever was eating him up, and she was much too close to his madness here. She veered away, seeking distance from his wild eyes, putting the bed between them.

'Do you realise what you're saying? You've just accused Grace of murder. You can't be serious.'

'I've never been more serious about anything in my life. She did it. She murdered Zoë. And I'm going to make damned sure she doesn't get the same opportunity with Olympia.'

His chest heaved under his dark and dangerous visage, his broad naked chest expanding rapidly with each sharp intake of air, emphasising the width of his shoulders and the power of his muscular torso all over, all the way down, down to where the skin disappeared beneath the denim. She swallowed.

Even now, even while he was accusing someone she looked up to more than anyone else in the world, even despite all that, she could hardly tear her eyes away. He looked like some supremely powerful predator, ready to spring, ready for the kill.

She battled to drag her eyes higher, refusing to think about what lay under that worn denim, what they'd been doing before the craziness had begun. Because if he was the hunter, then she was the prey— and he'd already feasted tonight. She'd as good as served herself up to him.

And yet, from what his words revealed, it had never been about her. Everything had been about Grace from the start! He'd been at the Gala not to meet Jade, as he'd said, but to feed some sick vendetta.

And she'd been caught up in his madness, had fallen victim to his rich magnetism, letting him keep her in his bed, letting him make love to her all those times.

Sickness pressed urgently in her throat—a vile taste that rebuked her for her own naïveté. How could she ever have believed she was falling in love with him? She'd been so gullible, so pathetically flattered by this man's interest. Just like before. Just like the last time. And this time she'd even managed to convince herself that he cared for her too.

Maybe she was the one with the problem.

Maybe she was the one who was mad.

His eyes trapped hers and flared, as if he knew what

she'd been thinking, what she'd been trying to forget, and knew that she didn't have a chance.

She willed her mouth to speak, to form the words that would indicate her silence had been more productive than merely used for a close inspection of his body.

'I'm sorry for what happened to your fiancée—'

He snorted his disbelief.

'Hear me out!' she insisted, holding up her hand to stall his protest. 'I don't care if you don't believe me, but if you expect me to believe *you*, you'd better start making some sense. How is Grace supposed to have carried out this so-called ''murder''?'

For a few moments he said nothing, continuing to stare across at her with such potent force that she could almost feel the power of his hurt. Could it be true? Could Grace have done something so terribly wrong that a patient had died? She didn't want to believe it, but at the back of her mind the increased frequency of legal action against her, the numerous settlements, all niggled at her certainty.

No. It couldn't be true.

'Well?' she pressed. 'You're making serious accusations against the most famous cosmetic surgeon in the country. Surely you don't expect me to believe you simply because you've managed to engineer me into your bed? You need to give me something concrete. What is it you think happened? What makes you so sure that Grace killed Zoë?'

His eyes glinted as they narrowed, a muscle twitching in his cheek. Then he jammed his fingers into his jeans pockets and turned towards the window, gazing out over the sea. It was some seconds more before he spoke, and when he did his voice was as flat and calm as the moonlit ocean beyond.

'It was four years ago. We were due to get married in three months. Zoë had never been overweight, but she'd started dieting for the wedding. Everyone—her family and I—thought it was just normal dieting, that she was just trying to look good for the wedding pictures. We didn't realise how thin she'd become. And still she kept on exercising for hours every day, hardly eating a thing.

'We were worried she was becoming anorexic. I told her that I couldn't marry her as she was; she was too fragile and she needed to get help. When she told me she'd booked into a clinic, I thought it was to get treatment for her condition.'

He sighed, pushing back his shoulders and stretching his neck. 'But instead she'd booked in for liposuction. And your wondrous Dr Della-Bosca made sure she'd never have a weight problem again.'

Chills crawled down her spine. 'Something went wrong?'

'You could say that. She was released after the surgery, and she checked herself into a hotel because she couldn't go home as she was. Progressively, she felt worse and worse. She rang the clinic twice, only to be told each time that the pain was normal. The third time she rang it was Della-Bosca herself who told her to stop wasting her time.'

Breath hissed through Jade's teeth. Surely Grace would never say such a thing to a client in pain?

'In desperation,' Loukas continued, 'she called her mother. She was out of it for much of the time, but she told her everything. By the time her mother and the paramedics found her, she was dead.'

'Oh, my God,' Jade whispered. 'And you believe that if she'd received attention earlier she might have lived?'

'I *know* she would have lived. And I know that it was Della-Bosca who killed her. The liposuction needle apparently pierced her abdominal cavity. It might have been peritonitis on the death certificate, but it was Della-Bosca who was holding that needle. It was Della-Bosca who murdered my Zoë.'

'It was an accident. A horrible accident.'

He wheeled around. 'No! It was no accident. She operated on a woman so wasted she could hardly stand up by herself. And instead of helping her, like she should have done, she fed Zoë's self-doubts and insecurities. She should have turned her away, but there was no way she would turn away Zoë's money.'

'I can't believe it. Grace isn't like that. You make out like she's some kind of mercenary. And she would never have operated if she hadn't thought it was necessary.' Yet even as Jade said the words she remembered another girl, another batch of operations scheduled, and the twinge in the back of her mind that something wasn't quite right. What had Grace said? *Satisfy her now and you'll have a client for life.* Had that been her reasoning with Zoë? So that even if she'd been anorexic Grace would have agreed to her request for surgery?

She shivered. It was too ghastly, too far-fetched. Grace wasn't like that, not normally. And it had been Grace herself who had saved Jade from a life not worth living. She'd been the one person who'd made her life possible when everyone else had given up trying.

'Loukas, I know you're hurting, but you have to remember the good work Grace does—look at the foundation, and the countless children's lives that will be improved. Just think of those children—no more will they have to hide their features in shadow; no more will they have to look at the ground so they avoid the looks from passers-by. Do you have any idea how that feels? To see the shock, then the horror and, finally, worst of all, the pity.

'It's Grace who gives those children a reason to wake up in the morning, to feel good about themselves and to hold their heads up high. So she might not be perfect—who is?—but I can't believe this picture you paint of her.'

She shook her head, this time with more authority. 'I can't believe it. Besides, there must have been an inquest. That would have cleared everything up.'

He snorted his disapproval. 'Zoë was dead. Della-Bosca's lawyers made the most of her slinking off to a hotel—said that she'd brought about her own death.'

'And the phone calls?'

'The hotel records supported the three calls to the clinic, but her mother's evidence wasn't accepted. They claimed Zoë would have been too close to death by the time she was found to have been coherent. And the clinic gave a totally different account of those calls, as you'd expect. In the end nobody was found responsible. No charges were laid.'

After the turbulence of their earlier argument, the air now seemed strangely still around them. Loukas stood there, watching her, his eyes almost empty, and in spite of the way he'd treated her, in spite of the way he'd used her to get to Grace, Jade's heart still wanted to go out to him.

It was no wonder he felt so strongly. He'd been cheated of his bride three months from their wedding—cheated of their future together. But nothing he could do would bring her back—least of all attacking Grace. He had to be made to see that.

She moved across the room to him, laying her hand on his arm.

'You went through a dreadful experience. It's not surprising that you have trouble accepting the findings, but you have to. You have to move on. Zoë would have wanted that.'

He shrugged off her hand as if it was some annoying insect and moved past her, picking up a shirt and hauling it on.

'I don't have to accept the findings. I know Grace killed Zoë and I'm going to make sure she doesn't touch my sister—with or without your help.'

'This is crazy, Loukas. Grace is nothing like you're making out. You don't know her like I do. She's a good woman.'

'If she's such a good woman,' he said, his words assured as he surveyed her, his eyes as polished and hard as the sheet of glass in the window behind him, 'then why the hell did she attempt Zoë's operation while she was stoned?'

CHAPTER EIGHT

SHE reeled from this latest accusation, fury turning molten inside her. Enough of trying to placate the man. This was going too far!

'That's an outright lie!'

'Is it? Were you there?'

'Were you?' she snapped back.

He smiled. 'Nice try. No, but I have proof. I tracked down the theatre nurse who was there that night. She confronted Della-Bosca over her drug use after that operation and found herself unemployed and on the receiving end of a considerable amount of cash to ensure she took a very long holiday and kept her mouth shut.'

'If this is true, why didn't she go to the police?'

'She was too scared—of Della-Bosca and the police. I tracked her down, only to have her die in an interstate collision the day before I was to meet with her and take her to the police.'

'And that, I take it,' she said, unable to resist the opportunity to show his case up for the fanciful supposition it was, 'was down to Grace as well?'

His eyes told her he half believed it.

'You're not serious?'

He shook his head. 'There's no proof.'

'And likewise you have no proof that Grace is guilty.'

'I believe what the theatre nurse told me.'

'You'd rather believe someone who wasn't honest enough to go to the police in the first place? Doesn't that tell you something about her from the start? I don't believe what she said for a minute. Grace doesn't do drugs. Don't you'd think I'd know if she did? How can it be that I've never heard any of these stories?'

'Because your charming doctor friend has paid to hush them up, same as she's done every time. Paid to hush up the woman rendered blind after a failed eyelid lift. Paid to hush up the girl who caught her snorting a line of coke in her office. Paid—'

'Stop it!' Jade yelled, her hand clutching the air. 'I don't believe it—any of it.'

He had her arms in his hands. He'd crossed the room so fast she hadn't realised. 'You don't believe it? Or you just don't like to think your cosy partner has been found out? It must be some team effort, covering up for all her mistakes. Is that why you had to invent the foundation—to provide more funds for her drug use, to provide more hush money to cover up her mistakes?'

She was thrashing in his arms, trying to get free. 'I'm not listening to any more of this. Let me go!'

His fingers squeezed tighter on her arms. 'And as for not knowing—I think you know a lot more about your good doctor than you let on.'

He dropped his grip on her, almost thrusting her away from him. She turned away, rubbing where his fingers had bitten down deep into her flesh.

'And if I did, why the hell would I tell you now? None of this makes sense, and I'm not going to contribute anything to this sick vendetta of yours.'

'Don't you understand anything?' he said, lurching forwards again. 'This is much more important than some mere vendetta!'

She recoiled momentarily and then, when she realised he wasn't reaching out to hold her again, she sighed, a long ragged sigh, shaking her head.

'You couldn't save Zoë so you're desperate to save a sister who doesn't want to be rescued. And you'll pull down anyone who gets in your way. What are you trying to prove, Loukas? Zoë died in obviously tragic circumstances, but she's gone. Hunting down Grace and ruining her career isn't going to bring her back for you. Can't you see that? If I wasn't so angry about what you're trying to do, I think I'd feel sorry for you.'

'I don't want your pity!'

She spun back to face him. 'Then what do you want? Do you expect me to help you on this crazy quest of yours? Is that what these last three nights were about? Did you think that once you'd got me into bed I'd only too readily spill everything I know about Grace's seedy underside? Is that what you thought? Well, okay, you being such a red-hot lover, I'll fall for it. I'll give you the goods. I'll tell you everything I know. Are you ready for this? Nothing. Zip. *Nada*. Do you understand? There is nothing to tell.'

Cold fire marked his features, the veins of his neck corded and pumping fury.

'I'll tell you what I understand. I thought you were different. Over these last few days I've thought there was just a chance you weren't like her. But I was wrong. You're two of a kind. You belong together in your black magic world, turning out your plastic clients and your Barbie doll lookalikes, living off people's insecurities and spreading fakery and artifice like a disease, like a weeping sore. And you're the biggest fake,' he continued with barely a pause. 'Because you pretend not to know or to see what's right in front of you.'

'I can't see what isn't there!'

'Still pretending,' he snorted. 'You're so fake you can't see straight. Or is that what happens when you've been under the knife too many times—you can't recognise the truth any more? Which bits of you are real, I wonder? And which are fake? That nose? Those breasts?'

'What are you talking about now? None of me is fake!'

He laughed. 'Sure. You've even dispensed with your accent so that nobody can tell who you are or where you're from. That's not fake? Face it, Jade, you have the services of the goddess of the cosmetic surgery world at your disposal. Don't expect me to believe you've never taken advantage of a slight nip and tuck.'

'Actually,' she said, turning to recover her clothes from where they'd been scattered over the floor, 'I'm past caring what you believe.'

'So deny it, then. Deny you've ever had a cosmetic procedure.'

She'd turned back, her mouth ready to snap back a retort in the negative, when she stopped herself short. Of course she'd had cosmetic procedures. First the botched attempts to remove the birthmark from her torso, and then the skilled hand of Grace finally ridding her of the mark from her face and neck.

So instead of answering she turned away with the bundle of clothes in her arms, heading for the *en suite* bathroom.

'I'm leaving,' she said. 'Don't bother seeing me out. I'll call a cab.'

Mayor Goldfinch's limo was parked in the driveway when Jade finally arrived home. She cursed silently under her breath. Even without all that had happened tonight the thought of seeing the Mayor made her feel sick to the stomach. His repulsive behaviour that night at the Gala was unforgivable—his betrayal of Grace a black mark that could never be removed.

And yet Mayor Goldfinch was only here tonight because she hadn't yet told Grace what she'd stumbled upon in the library. So wasn't her own silence just as damning? Why hadn't she had the guts to tell Grace what she'd seen? Why hadn't she at least warned the woman who was supposed to mean more to her than anyone that the man she was involved with wasn't to be taken at face value?

Damn the man, and damn his presence!

Now there would be no chance to warn Grace tonight about Loukas's bizarre claims against her. And she had to talk to her. She *needed* to talk to her. Because on the long ride home Loukas's evil claims had started to work on her psyche, had started to worm their way into her beliefs, and there were some things that might almost make sense—*would* almost make sense if you were as grief-crazed with loss as Loukas.

There *had* been a large number of negligence cases against the clinic settled out of court in the last few years. It might simply be a reflection of the US being a litigious society, as she'd so long assumed, but what if she was wrong? Was it really a sign of something more sinister? What if there really was another reason for the uncomfortable number of cases that had ended in settlements?

Grace's unexpected cynicism about operating on Pia still irritated her sensibilities. Was the pursuit of money really that important to her?

But Grace could put her mind to rest on all of these issues. And she would.

Because the alternative was just too hard to think about, too impossible to be true.

At least she could be certain of one thing. Grace didn't do drugs. She knew Grace wouldn't be so crazy as to risk her whole career. But still she needed to talk to her. And the Mayor's presence meant that she wouldn't get a chance tonight.

Quietly she crossed the entrance foyer, heading for the stairs.

'Jade!' Grace's voice trailed out from one of the rooms, stopping her in her tracks. 'Come in. It's so good you're here. I have something to tell you.'

Jade suppressed a curse, taking a deep breath and tucking the stray strands of her hair behind her ears as she tried not to think about the last time she'd seen Mayor Goldfinch—tried not to think about what he'd been doing and with whom. She plastered what she hoped would pass for a smile on her face, and entered the room.

Mayor Goldfinch beamed at her and pulled a bottle

of Cristal champagne from a silver ice bucket, pouring into an empty flute. Uneasy prickles started climbing up her spine. Why the hell would they be drinking champagne? Unless...

'You're the first to know,' the Mayor said, pressing the flute into her hand with a beefy smile that turned her stomach almost as much as his words filled her with apprehension. She looked to Grace, hoping she was wrong, hoping she'd misinterpreted what this private little party was all about. But Grace smiled on, her eyes starry, her face radiant.

'The first to know what?' she asked, trying to garner the appropriate amount of enthusiasm for the game as they eked out the details.

'The first to hear our wonderful news,' Grace explained, beaming. 'We're going to be married.'

Oh, God, poor Grace. Not only did Grace have Loukas Demakis breathing down her neck, but now she was marrying this sleazebag of a man. She had no idea what she was letting herself in for.

And what made it worse was that Jade was going to have to be the one who told her. There was no way she could avoid telling her now. Grace would have to be told what she had seen that night in the library.

Rapidly losing the battle to grip onto her smile, Jade managed a brief, 'Congratulations,' before taking a sip from her flute. Anything to save her from saying something she might regret later. She wished mightily that the superb champagne was a better contest for the bitter taste in her mouth right now.

'Absolutely—and I sure deserve a deal of congratulating. She sure made me sweat it out, waiting for her decision.'

Grace laughed, slipping her arm through the Mayor's. 'Goodness! It was only a few days. He actually asked me at the foundation Gala on Saturday night as he was leaving—wasn't that sweet?'

Jade had to get out of there, and fast. She whispered a hurried but honest excuse that she'd come home early because she was feeling off-colour before she bolted to her bathroom just in time to lose the contents of her stomach. Far too much was happening tonight for her body to be able to cope with something as pedestrian as digesting food.

She sat there in the dark for a long time afterwards, wondering about—angsting over—what she should do. The Mayor's behaviour was beyond repulsive, his actions utterly reprehensible. How could he have behaved that way—committing an act like that with some wannabe actress barely out of her teenage years—on the very night he'd gone on to ask Grace to marry him? What kind of man was he? And what kind of lousy husband would he make?

Her heart went out to Grace. How could she tell her? How could she dash her dreams?

She sucked in a deep breath as she collapsed onto her bed, her battered stomach bruised and aching but at least feeling more stable. Now it was just her mind that churned sickeningly.

Only one thing was clear—Grace was going to need her support more than ever once she was told the truth. And Jade would give her every bit of support she could, and she'd make doubly sure that people like Loukas Demakis couldn't touch her. His mad accusations and his bizarre need for revenge for the sad tragedy that had taken Zoë from him were the last thing Grace needed right now.

She squeezed her eyes shut as she curled into a tight ball on the coverlet.

She didn't want to think about Loukas!

At least not without anger. He'd used her as a means to get to Grace—to destroy Grace—and he'd told such hideous lies, made such crazy claims. It was okay to be angry.

Anger was what she wanted.

Anger was what she needed.

White-hot anger that would scorch the truth of his actions into her consciousness with an acid burn—only that way could she let herself think about Loukas.

Only that would take her mind off this huge sense of loss, this overwhelming sense of betrayal.

He'd made himself out to be a different person than he was. He'd made out that his advances to her had actually meant something when they hadn't. He'd tricked her into having dinner with him, tricked her by promising one million dollars to the foundation. And yet he didn't care anything for those children with birth deformities, the kids with bone or facial imperfections who had grown up being freaks and outcasts in their own families and their own communities. The kids whose families couldn't afford the fares to get them to the clinic, let alone the cost of surgery. The kids who otherwise didn't have a hope.

He'd found the one thing to ensure she'd agree to go with him, the ideal bait to hook her with, and he'd used it unconscionably to bend her to his will. And she'd gone along with it. She'd fallen for the bait and in the end he hadn't even had to reel her in. She'd all but wrapped the fishing line around her throat herself. She'd offered herself to him on a plate.

One million dollars. The only good thing to come out of this whole sordid affair.

Her eyes snapped open in the darkened room. *Assuming he'd made the promised donation!*

She hadn't followed up on the delivery of the cheque—hadn't asked him about it in the heady glow of their lovemaking. Why would she, when she'd trusted him completely?

What a complete fool she'd been!

'Grace, we have to talk.' Jade stood nervously in the sunny breakfast room, her hands clammy, her head pounding. She'd been relieved to see the Mayor's limousine gone this morning, even though it meant she couldn't put off what she had to do.

The older woman glanced at her watch and finished her early-morning cup of espresso. 'Better make it snappy, then, Jade. We've both got a full list today. Mind you,' she added, peering over the newspaper at her, 'I must say you still look a little peaky. Still not feeling well? Do you want a cup of coffee?'

She shook her head, 'No, thanks. It's not that, Grace. It's actually about your engagement.'

Grace put the paper down. 'I was so delighted to see you home early last night. But it was sad you had to rush off like that. Charles was quite worried about you.'

'I'm sorry,' Jade said, her eyes finding it hard to stick on the older woman's.

'It doesn't matter. As it happens I need to talk to

you too. Charles thinks we should have a big party to celebrate, and he was wondering whether you might be able to help—you did such a fabulous job organising the Gala.'

'Grace, I really don't know if that's such a good idea.'

'You're too modest, you know. I thought it was an inspired idea. I know it was such a lot of work for you, but couldn't you do it as a favour to me?'

Jade hauled in a breath and dropped herself into the closest chair. 'Look, Grace, are you sure about marrying Mayor Goldfinch?'

'What on earth do you mean? Of course I'm sure. Why? Do you have a problem with it?'

'Well, I'm really worried about something I saw at the Gala, but I'm not sure how to tell you. It's about the Mayor.'

Her face hardened. 'What about the Mayor?'

'I saw him—at the Gala—with Rachael Delaney.'

Grace's face looked blank. 'And?'

Jade licked her lips. 'And...they were making love.'

'What? Oh, Jade, no way!' Grace shook her head, lifting herself from her chair as she folded the newspaper on the table into four. 'Why on earth would you want to tell me something ridiculous like that?'

'Because I saw them.'

'Well, you must have seen someone else. Because there's no way he'd be having it off with anyone—least of all Rachael. She's just a child.'

'I'm sorry, Grace.'

'Well, I don't believe it. And why wouldn't you have told me before if you had seen him? Why wait until now?'

'I didn't want to hurt you! But when he said you were getting married I couldn't let you go through with it. I couldn't keep quiet any more. Can't you see? That's why I felt so sick last night—I was upset for you.'

Grace was shaking her head, her hands smoothing down her slim-fitting skirt. 'I don't believe it. Charles is a total gentleman. And I can't for the life of me work out why you'd want to say such a thing.' Then she looked up, her eyes narrowing. She gave a little mocking laugh. 'You're not jealous of me, are you, Jade? Because I'm getting married?'

'No. Of course not!'

'Not even just a little bit? Maybe it's Charles you want for yourself, perhaps? Or are you jealous of me finding love when you've got no chance? Not with that scar—not around this town.'

Grace's words sliced into her psyche like razor-blades, deep and painful and unnecessary. 'No. You've got it all wrong.'

'Or are you worried you'll lose your apartment and have to move out after the wedding?' Grace hesitated, her tongue poised on her top lip. 'Actually, that's not such a bad idea, come to think of it. Maybe it would be for the best. I won't want you here with Charles if you're going to say such things.'

'But Grace—'

'No, Jade. I've made up my mind. I think it's time you moved on.'

Jade dropped her office phone back onto its base, momentarily confused after speaking to the bank manager. But after the trauma of her meeting with Grace it was no wonder she couldn't think straight.

Somehow she'd negotiated the traffic and driven herself to the clinic, and somehow she had to get through today without thinking about everything that was falling to pieces around her.

But first she had to hold her raw nerves together and deal with a new problem. She'd had the bank manager repeat the figure three times. She'd heard him right. The foundation's bank balance was lower—much lower—than what she'd expected after the last trustees' meeting, and the six-hundred-thousand-dollar figure told her one thing for certain—no way had Loukas deposited the promised funds.

In scorching anger she reached for her phone again. Right this minute it didn't matter that he'd deceived her. It didn't matter that they'd parted on such terms. And it didn't mean a thing that her argument with Grace might mean she wouldn't be around to see the money put to good use. The most important thing right now was that scores of children would be denied the help of the foundation because Loukas had lied to her.

Damned if she'd let him cheat those children!

He answered on the second ring.

'We had a deal,' she snapped.

A heavy silence followed her statement.

Then, 'What of it?'

Her fury increased tenfold. 'I expected you to follow through with your end of the bargain, regardless of anything that happened between us. That's "what of it".'

'You're talking about the money?'

'Of course I'm talking about the money! You promised one million dollars for the foundation!'

'And I take it you believe I didn't follow through on my promise?'

'I *know* you didn't.'

Another moment's silence. 'I see.'

'Is that all you have to say? "I see"?'

'Well, from your tone I take it you wouldn't be likely to believe me anyway if I told you I delivered the cheque to your legal people myself?'

'Don't give me that. The money should be there. It's clearly not.'

'Then…might I suggest there may well be another reason why the funds have gone missing?'

'Don't you *dare* start that again! I heard enough of your lies and accusations last night. You're not getting out of your commitment that easily.'

'I assume that means Grace has denied all knowledge of what's happened to the funds. That's *if* you've even consulted Grace.'

'Grace has nothing to do with your failure to deposit the money.'

'So you haven't asked her? You should. She might have something very enlightening to say.'

Jade shook her head, more at herself than at the arrogant voice on the other end. No way was she going to be swayed by his lies and diversions.

'This is about you,' she said into the receiver, 'not Grace. And you made a promise—one million dollars for the foundation if I had dinner with you. I kept my end of the bargain.' *With interest,* she thought bitterly, resenting herself for the way she'd fallen so readily into his bed, but determined not to let her stupidity deter her from what she had to do. 'Now I expect you to keep yours.'

'I'll sort it out.'

'Make sure you do—today!'

She broke the connection, her hands trembling, all of her shaking, as she gave herself up to the aftermath of the phone call.

Damn the man!

The clock on the wall told her she had less than thirty minutes to get herself under control before her first patient. She searched her desk for her schedule, trying to replace the chaos of her mind with order. Her eyes found the list, registering the first name with a sense of creeping unease.

Pia Kovac.

Why, today of all days, did she have to be scheduled for laser surgery?

Reluctantly she reached for the file.

CHAPTER NINE

SOMETHING was wrong. There was a disturbance coming from inside the surgical rooms. Jade heard a clatter, a crash, and then a theatre sister pushed out through the doors, the expression on her face a mixture of fear and panic.

'Dr Ferraro!' she called, her eyes lighting on hers. 'Thank God you're here. Come quickly.'

'What is it?' Jade asked, breaking into a run behind the turning nurse.

'Something's wrong with Dr Della-Bosca,' she replied breathlessly, pushing open the swing doors through to the scrub room and into the prep room beyond. 'She thinks she's doing a breast augmentation, but you're down for laser surgery on this patient. When I tried to tell her, she went mad.'

Oh, my God!

Jade took one look inside the room and froze as she took in the bizarre tableau in front of her. Boxes of medical supplies and instruments were scattered all over the floor of the room, in the centre of which stood Grace, felt-tipped pen in hand, calmly marking out lines on the naked breasts of the blonde girl lying on the trolley.

The girl seemed completely out of it, and fear cranked up inside Jade—she wasn't down for a premed before her laser treatment, so what the hell had Grace given her?

But before she could take care of Pia, it was Grace's condition that worried her more right now. The apparent calmness with which she continued with her geometrical markings was at complete odds with the scene of devastation all around her.

'What's going on?' Jade asked, knowing for all Grace's apparent air of normality that something was desperately, frighteningly wrong. Quickly she turned to the theatre sister, mouthing the word 'security' and seeing her brief nod before she backed purposefully out of the room.

Then she looked back at Grace, and what she saw in Grace's eyes made fear and anxiety come together inside her like a tangled, stinking clump of seaweed, pushed up by the tide and left to decompose on the shore.

'Everything's fine,' Grace assured her. 'We don't need you yet.'

'But Pia is my patient this morning.'

Grace looked up from her work and over at Jade. 'You're not even gowned up. I might as well make a start if you're not ready.'

She had to be ill! Her behaviour was too far out of the ordinary, yet too calm for all that had happened between them this morning.

Then Jade reassessed the tiny pinpricks of the older woman's eyes peering out at her, and in one heart-sinking moment the tangled seaweed ball inside her congealed into something much more knowing.

Drugs. While everything she knew about Grace begged her to be wrong, her brain screamed that there was no question that this woman was under the influence of a mind-altering substance. She'd taken something—most likely some kind of opiate—to make her so calm and make her pupils look so unnaturally pin-prick-sized. But from the way she was behaving, the way she was so far out of control, she must have misjudged and overdosed herself.

Oh, Grace, she thought, blaming herself, her heart heavy for her friend even as concern for Pia was foremost in her mind, *what have I done?*

She moved closer to the woman, keeping a steady eye on the encouraging rise and fall of Pia's chest, fuelled by the welcome sounds of commotion outside. Help was coming. 'Grace, I don't think that's such a good idea. I think you might want to come with me. Let's go and sit in your office.'

'What are you talking about? You don't tell me what to do. You think you're so good, so perfect. Sweet, perfect Dr Ferraro. But you'd be nothing without me—nothing! Mind you,' Grace continued, waving the blue pen around as if it was a wand, 'you do have some good ideas from time to time. That foundation idea of yours was the best one you had. All that lovely money. All for me.'

'No! That money is to help the children who can't afford surgery.'

'Such a clever plan! I knew I kept you around for a reason.'

'Grace, you're not well,' Jade persisted, not believing what she was hearing, trying to ignore the stinging remarks in her concern for her friend. 'Have you taken something?'

Grace laughed then, a hideous cackle that chilled Jade's blood. 'Of course I've damned well taken something! Everybody in this town does. How else do you think we make it through the day? You really are a hick, aren't you? I should have left you back there where you came from. I never should have bothered with you.'

All that was left of her feelings for Grace shrivelled up and died. This wasn't a one-off, triggered by her earlier revelation of Mayor Goldfinch's infidelity. This was a regular event. Grace was a user.

'But you're not well. Let me help you—*please*!'

'I'm perfectly well! Get out of my way so I can operate.'

Grace focused her attention once more on drawing blue lines on Pia's bare breasts.

Jade took advantage of her bowed head and, knowing Security would soon be with them, moved again—close enough to reach out and...

With one fluid movement she lifted the pen from Grace's hands. The shock in the older woman's eyes and the reaction of her fingers were made all the duller by whatever drug was pumping through her veins.

Then the doors burst open—but it was not the security guards she'd been expecting. The first person into the room stopped dead, his six-foot-four frame coming to a halt just inside the doors, his face like thunder. His granite-hard eyes rapidly took in the room, flicking over the two woman standing next to the trolley and widening with shock and recognition when they encountered the gowned occupant beneath them.

'Loukas—' Jade said, totally bewildered as she attempted to find words to explain what was happening even while still holding onto the pen she'd taken from Grace's hands, as if she'd been the one wielding it.

'What the hell are you doing to my sister?'

CHAPTER TEN

JADE'S world collapsed around her in the following few days. The clinic was closed and Grace was whisked away by the authorities, with moves already underway to have her deregistered.

And Jade was next in line. She spent hours answering seemingly endless and repetitive questions from the police, 'assisting them with their enquiries', as they so diplomatically put it.

What did she know of Grace's drug use? Who was her supplier? Who had financial responsibility for the clinic and the foundation bank accounts?

She answered as best she could, her spirits in a slump, her voice a monotone. And the more they asked, the more she realised how stupid she'd been, how hopelessly naïve, how easily she'd missed the signals about what was going on around her—like Grace's constant interest in the accounts and her late hours working into the night.

Because she hadn't wanted to see them—hadn't let herself see them.

Because her stupid ill-placed loyalty had blinded her.

How she made it through the battery of one round of questioning after another she didn't know. Maybe it was because she was numb, so deeply in shock over what had happened that it felt as if nothing could ever touch her again. And that was good. She didn't want to feel.

Because then she couldn't feel pain.

At last the police decided that she had helped them as much as she could and that there was no reason to hold her any longer. She was free to go.

Escorted by an officer, she was waiting for the lift that would come and return her to the outside world when the doors of one of the other interview rooms opposite opened. She almost looked away—until she saw who spilled out, and then she gasped.

Flanked by two officers, Grace walked, head held high, even though her arms were handcuffed behind her. But, despite the angle of her chin, she looked suddenly old, with dark circles under her eyes and her skilfully raised cheekbones suspending hollowed flesh beneath.

Across the waiting area their eyes met. Grace's glinted coldly in the glow from the artificial office lighting above.

Jade involuntarily took a step forward, her lips turning up instinctively, before she realised where she was and why they were both there. Her smile slid away again. But she wanted to say something—just to let her know that if Grace needed her...

'Grace—' she began.

The officer alongside her put his hand on her arm to keep her where she was, but she'd already stopped at the ice-cold glare from Grace's eyes.

'You *bitch*!' Grace said, her voice so sharp it cut the air between them like a scalpel. 'You did this to me! I made you what you are, and this is how you repay me? I should have let you rot in that Outback town of yours. I should have burned that birthmark black!'

The lift doors opened and Jade stumbled in, waiting for what seemed like an eternity before the doors hissed closed and the lift began its grinding descent, gradually blocking out the sounds of the screaming woman, although the echoes of her words and the painful reminder of her early life continued to ring loudly in her ears long after she'd left the building.

There was a crowd gathered outside the gates of the mansion—almost as if there was a party and everyone had been asked to park outside. But the cars weren't convertibles or coupés. These were trucks and vans with dishes and aerials on their roofs.

Uncertain, she asked the cab driver to pull up several houses away, where she stood on the kerb for a few seconds, wondering how she'd get into the house without being noticed.

'You gonna pay me, lady?'

She blinked and paid the fare automatically in response, not thinking that she'd be better off getting right back in and finding somewhere else to stay. By the time she'd worked out that it was a crowd of reporters swarming around the entrance to the mansion the cab was already disappearing into the distance.

She looked around. The street was otherwise as it always was—quiet, serene, and a haven from downtown traffic. There was little chance of another cab passing.

Someone in the distance called out, 'It's her!' and

suddenly the pack was in motion, picking up cameras and other equipment, heading straight for her.

'Dr Ferraro!' they called. 'Dr Ferraro!'

She knew instinctively she should run. She knew instinctively she should hide. But there was nowhere to go, nowhere to run—and, just as her mind felt frozen, her feet seemed welded to the spot. It was all she could do to watch the hungry pack draw closer.

Then, from somewhere close behind her, came the roar of an engine and a squeal of tyres, and a voice yelled out, 'Get in!'

Loukas?

She looked around. The passenger door of the car hung open and he was waiting inside for her to join him. She tried to shake her head. None of this could be happening. Why would Loukas be here? Surely not to save her? Not after what he'd thought about her from the start. Not after all she'd done to stop him.

And all the while the pack drew closer still, the leaders now only seconds away

'Come on! Get in,' he urged. 'They'll tear you to pieces.'

And something in her mind clicked into place. After spending the best part of two days being interviewed by the police, the last thing she could face right now was reporters jamming their cameras into her face, wanting more of the same, wanting every last sordid detail of the scandal that was rocking Hollywood to its core.

Whatever fate Loukas had planned for her, at least he could save her from that.

She slid down into the seat alongside him with the first reporter only metres away. But she didn't close the door. She didn't have to. The car's powerful acceleration took care of that, swinging the wide door closed as Loukas steered away from the kerb and past the ribbon of disgruntled reporters, cheated of their prey.

She took a deep breath and settled back into the luxurious leather seat, finding the familiar smell of his car much more to her liking than the stained cab she'd just exited. Until she realised what it was that she liked about it—it bore the imprint of Loukas's own signature scent.

And suddenly she didn't feel comfortable. She didn't want to think about that side of Loukas. She didn't want to be reminded of the times they'd spent in this car on their way to the beach house, anticipating what was to follow, their sexual excitement mounting as they drew closer to their destination, the hunger between them building.

Dammit! She couldn't afford to think about those nights.

Because they were gone. Just the same as her strident defence of Grace—blown to smithereens by the truth, the real truth that Loukas had known all along and that she had fought so hard against the whole time.

She pushed her head back into the leather-upholstered headrest as the enormity of one simple fact worked its way clear from the fog of her mind. *She'd* been the one who was wrong.

It was Loukas who had been right all along.

Her throat tightened, her mouth ashen. How could she even start to admit it?

How the hell could she begin to tell him how much

she was sorry? How much she wished she'd listened to him instead of blocking out everything he said as if his words were poisoned? His warnings should have made some sort of sense, given she'd been starting to have her own concerns about Grace's hunger for money. Instead she'd blocked it out with walls made of her loyalty to Grace. Her stupid, ill-placed loyalty that had been shattered until it tumbled down and now lay in ruins around her.

She turned her head a fraction and glanced at his profile. His jaw looked set, his eyes rigidly glued to the traffic. Hardly a surprise. He was bound to be angry with her. She hadn't believed his claims and then she'd all but accused him of cheating the foundation out of a million dollars. And that was all before he'd found her standing over his sister, preparing to operate, as if she *was* the one who was crazed.

She had to be crazy.

But suddenly being crazy seemed the easy option. No longer did she recognise her world. It had tilted way off axis, turning truth to lies and lies to truth and heroes to villains. And still none of it made sense. She was a stranger in a strange new world.

Even the fact that it was Loukas who had come to her rescue tonight was crazy. He was the last person she would have expected to whisk her away from more embarrassment and more pain. He must hate the very sight of her.

So she'd ensure he didn't need to put up with her company any longer than was absolutely necessary. She took a deep breath.

'Thank you,' she said finally, sounding too loud as she fractured the silence between them. But she owed him at least her thanks for getting her away from the reporters—even if being trapped with him in his car was hardly what she'd call sanctuary. 'You can drop me at a hotel anywhere convenient.'

He only grunted in response and kept right on driving. She turned her head away, determined not to be affected by his obvious distaste for her. But when they'd passed an entire strip of hotels she turned to him again. 'I said you could let me out. What's wrong with any of these places?'

'You'd be tracked down by the media in ten minutes flat.'

'Look, I can take care of myself.'

'Which is what you were doing back there so impressively, no doubt.'

'Then where are you taking me?'

'Where do you think? Somewhere you'll be safe, and the last place they'll think to look for you.'

Panic welled up inside her. He couldn't be serious!

'No! Not the beach house. I won't go. You can't expect me to stay there.'

'You have no choice. Right now you have nowhere else to go,' he said, closing down the argument.

Loukas was garaging the car when she entered the living room. The first thing she noticed were the newspapers scattered on the coffee table, the headlines screaming out at her.

Fallen From Grace
The Deepest Cut
No Saving Grace
A Foundation of Evil

She picked up the least inflammatory-looking paper and skimmed the front-page article before dropping the newspaper back down on the table and sliding open the glass doors leading out to the deck.

The story was splashed all over every one of the papers, with the Demakis name everywhere, and yet for all that it looked as if it wouldn't do the Senator's chances in the upcoming primaries any harm at all.

Pia was clearly the helpless victim, with Loukas painted as the hero—saving her from disfigurement or death or maybe even both.

On the other hand Grace was portrayed as a crazed psycho who believed the myth built up around her so much that she actually thought herself to be a goddess—way above both other mere mortals and the law.

Maybe there was some truth in that, Jade acknowledged as she leant down and rested her forearms on the deck balustrade, relishing the tang of the fresh sea breeze after being stuck in the airless box of a police building answering questions for so long.

Grace had always loved the celebrity that came from being a vital part of the world of the rich and famous. She'd loved the buzz that came from being courted by the fabulously wealthy who needed to be fabulously beautiful as well. She'd wielded the power to change lives and fortunes in her hands. She'd been a goddess to them!

And now the scandal of Grace's undoing was causing shockwaves that were reverberating throughout Hollywood's celebrity circles—not to mention causing a great deal of appointment-rescheduling.

Thank God she was out of it for now. Thank God the clinic was closed and she could step back from this crazy industry. Because this wasn't what she'd had in mind when she'd come to LA. She'd wanted to make a difference for good, to help people make the most of their lives. And yet when she'd joined Grace's clinic all that had changed.

Sure, for a while it had been exhilarating, exciting, and she'd loved the pace of life and the challenge. But she hadn't been helping the people who needed it most, and if she hadn't been working with her very own heroine, planning for the future of the foundation, surely she would have thought about moving on.

The foundation. What a joke! There was no foundation. Not the way she'd wanted. There was a fund, to be sure. But just how Grace had planned to make use of that fund...

A noise behind her alerted her to Loukas's presence. She turned to see him standing stock-still in the doorway, his eyes calmly surveying her. She shivered as his cold eyes chilled the air around her. How long had he been there, watching her?

'Are you all right?' he asked, his voice flat and almost lifeless.

'Is that why you brought me here? To ensure that I was all right?' she responded, half wishing that he had, half hoping that he might have acted out of at least a modicum of concern for her welfare, even after everything that had happened.

It was insane, and yet it also seemed so important. Could he care for her? Just a little? After what they'd shared, surely there was something, some tiny residual shred of feeling for her?

'I brought you here so the reporters can't find you. What else?'

What else indeed? A bucket of cold water couldn't have doused her pathetic hopes more effectively. She had been insane to even think it. After all, right from the start he'd never acted out of concern for her. He'd only ever wanted her so he could use her against Grace.

All thoughts of wanting to apologise to him evaporated in an instant in the cold, hard light of his attitude.

His face tight, his voice sounding strained, he continued before she had a chance to get her simmering thoughts in order. 'I've put some fresh linen in the guestroom. I'll get someone to pick up some clothes for you in the morning. Goodnight.'

Then he was gone.

'Just how long do you plan on keeping me here?'

Loukas looked up from his newspaper, replacing a cup of coffee in its saucer with a low clatter. Jade was pacing behind the wide serving bench that separated the kitchen from the living area, her hands busy with each other as she paced, and turned, and paced some more. This was only her second morning at the beach house, and yet already her face looked tight and drawn.

Then he let himself do what he'd been avoiding doing all of yesterday, and let his eyes skim over the rest of her. Her curves were there, under her summer cut-offs and halter top, but she seemed, more angular in places. She'd lost weight.

He frowned. That was the last thing he wanted. 'Come and eat some breakfast. You look gaunt.'

'I'm not hungry.'

'You need to eat something.'

'How long?' She stopped pacing and turned to face him, her eyes pleading while at the same time resolute. 'The police said I was free to go. So how does that give you the right to kidnap me and lock me away?'

He raised his cup and took another slug of coffee. He needed the caffeine after two nights of trying—and failing miserably—to sleep half a dozen rooms away from where she lay. How many times had he imagined he heard her soft footfall coming down the hall? How often had he dozed off, half dreaming, half imagining that she was in his arms again, only to wake and find them empty or wrapped around twisted sheets?

And how many times had he been tempted to take those few short steps himself?

But that would serve no purpose now. She was only here so that he could protect Olympia. Nothing more.

But he didn't know how long it would take. All he knew was that already it seemed too long. So instead he asked, 'Have you read today's papers?'

She shook her head, tucking strands of loose hair behind her ears. She hadn't tied it back this morning, and the ends dusted the line of her bare neck and shoulders. Something inside him clenched, and he forced himself to drag his eyes away from the sensual marriage of bare skin and whispering hair.

'I can't bear to read any of it.'

'Mayor Goldfinch has been arrested. Seems he was hooking up with Della-Bosca to have access to the foundation's fund. They both wanted a slice of that pie. It looks like the end of that career.'

'Bastards! Both of them!' she said, so emphatically that he looked up in surprise. But jail was nothing more than they both deserved. And to think she'd felt sorry for Grace when she'd discovered what kind of man he really was!

'How could they steal money away from children's hopes and dreams like that?' she asked. 'How could they do that? And why did he even need to? He's already got a huge property development fortune.'

'Not any more. He's been losing money for years, living in debt and relying on cash flow, waiting for another big success to take him out of it. Della-Bosca was good at masking what she'd been doing with the foundation funds, but not that good. Once he found out about her misappropriation of funds, he demanded equal access to keep his mouth shut. Between the two of them the foundation didn't stand a chance.'

He watched her curiously for a few moments, and she wondered what he was thinking. No doubt he believed that she should be in jail too.

And then she remembered what she'd done that awful morning, before Grace's house of cards had collapsed around her, when she'd called Loukas demanding he pay up his promised one-million-dollar donation and keep his promise to the children.

Her eyes fell shut and she breathed deep on a long blink. Oh, God, no wonder everything was such a mess. She had forgotten completely about his money.

'Loukas,' she said, licking her lips, buying herself time as if it might find her some courage, 'I'm not happy with how you treated me—how you used me like you did. But there's one thing I need to apologise for. About the foundation.' She paused for a few moments then. 'You made that donation like you said, didn't you?'

'I told you I had.'

'And they stole it—along with the rest of the money?'

'So it appears.'

'Then I'm sorry. I was angry when I called you. I thought you hadn't paid...'

'You don't need to apologise,' he said, rising from his chair and turning towards the windows, hands on hips. 'It was your call that made me decide to confront Della-Bosca myself. That's why I was there. That's why I was lucky enough to find Olympia.'

And that was why he'd found Jade standing over his sister next to a madwoman, and looking for all the world as if *she* had been the one intending to operate. Her throat tightened. 'You know...I wasn't...'

'I know,' he said, his voice thick and strained, as if he was trying to keep it under control. And looked away, as if he would rather change the topic completely than continue this conversation.

Her tongue found her lips again, fighting a losing battle to keep them moist. She needed to press on. There were still more things she needed to say, whether or not he wanted to hear them. They had to be said before she changed her mind.

'And I'm sorry for not believing all those things you said about Grace too. You were right.'

He spun around in an instant and rounded the table towards her, ramming his fist into the air, his face masked with fury.

'Don't you think it's too late for that now? My sister could have been scarred for life, or worse—she could have been killed by that lunatic! And yet you did nothing—*nothing!*—to stop her!'

She took a step back, blinking at the sudden speed of his approach. He was right. She had done nothing. And it hardly seemed to matter now that it was because she had believed nothing could possibly be wrong.

He'd been such a champion for his sister, fighting both to save her and to avenge his late fiancée. What would it feel like to have someone fight so hard for you, to defend you so stridently, to care for you that much?

Did his sister know how lucky she was?

'H…How is Pia now? Do you know?'

He stopped, and dragged in some air, his fist slowly melting back into a hand as he battled to get his breathing under control. 'She's at home. Stella is looking after her—and Kurt, though I don't know how much good he'll be. I'm just hoping it will be a long while before she attempts any cosmetic surgery again.'

She smiled wanly. 'I'm glad she's okay. She seems a nice kid.'

His eyes hardened to stone. 'Exactly,' he hissed, moving closer to her. '*A kid.* And yet you were prepared to let that monster cut into her.'

'It wasn't like that.'

'No? It sure looked like it to me.'

'I even tried to talk Pia—*Olympia*—out of it. But she wouldn't listen to me. She was determined to go ahead with the surgery.'

He snorted his disbelief. 'Don't give me that!'

'It's the truth!'

'You can't make things any better for yourself, you know, so don't even bother trying.'

She swallowed back the lump in her throat, fighting the prick of tears that surged up at the injustice. Why had she even bothered to apologise to this brute? He wasn't prepared to accept anything from her, let alone the truth. 'Fine,' she said. 'You've never believed anything I've said. Why should what I say today be any different?'

'You're not the victim in all this, so don't make out like you are.'

'I want to leave,' she said, immediately gritting her teeth together in an effort to keep a hold over the burgeoning bubble of unshed tears that was swelling by the second. 'I'm going.'

'You're not going anywhere!'

'You can't keep me here!'

'Just watch me.'

'There's no need. You don't need to protect me any more.'

'You think I'm protecting you?'

'What do you mean? Isn't that why you brought me here? To protect me from the reporters?'

His only response was to blink.

'I don't care about the reporters,' she said. 'I can handle them myself.'

'That's exactly what I'm afraid of.'

'What do you mean?'

'How much do you think they'll give you for your story? I think they'd pay a fortune to get the goods from you—probably enough to tide you over while you search for some other laboratory to perform your sick experiments.'

'I don't believe you! You really think I'd sell my version of events to the highest bidder?'

His eyes dropped away. 'I can't afford to take any chances. So far the Demakis name has escaped being tainted by this scandal. But if someone were to give the press something adverse or embarrassing...'

'And you think I would? That's why you're holding me prisoner here—because I might lift some dirt on your precious family? So how long do you think you can keep me here—how long do you plan on keeping me silent? A week? A month? For ever?'

He slammed his fist against the wall. 'I don't want Olympia hurt any more than she has been!'

'And you don't believe me when I say I'd do nothing to hurt Pia? But why should that come as a surprise? Ever since we've met you've been only too happy to misjudge me. All the way along you've been happy to assume the worst.'

'What are you saying?'

'I'm saying you've never chosen to believe me over your own warped preconceived notions. Even when they're proved wrong, you still won't accept it. You assumed I was in with Grace from the start. You decided I was just as guilty. Were you disappointed when the police didn't lock me away? Would it have been easier for you if they'd kept me behind bars and thrown away the key—saved you the trouble?'

'Stop it!'

'Why should I? Why should I do anything you say? It's not as if you're the bastion of what's right and true in the world. Look at the way you treated me. You used me—lied to me—tricked me into sleeping with you so that I might spill what I knew about Grace. Well, the joke is on you, Loukas, because it was all for nothing. I didn't know anything. You went to all the trouble of bedding me for nothing! All that effort—totally wasted!'

And then he was upon her, his breath harsh on her face, the drumbeat of his heart a mere few inches away.

'I wouldn't call it a complete waste.'

CHAPTER ELEVEN

SUDDENLY his lips were on hers, hungry, punishing, his tongue seeking entry, his hands seemingly everywhere, ripping at her halter and her pants.

And the taste of Loukas in her mouth, the feel of his hands upon her, his body pressed next to hers was almost enough to make her forget what they'd been arguing about. Make her want to melt into his passionate embrace. Give herself up to his mind, and body-shattering onslaught.

Almost.

Summoning a strength of body and mind from somewhere, from the only place deep within that was untouched by the desire to let herself go, she pushed him away.

'No!'

Her hands flush on his chest, her breathing rough and edgy, she battled to stay calm. 'This didn't solve anything before, and it will solve even less now!'

She pushed with all her remaining strength, but the effort to shove him away had drained her and his hands felt like manacles on her arms.

'I don't want this!'

'I know you do,' he insisted, pressing the weight of his chest against her hands, his mouth seeking her lips once more.

'No. You're wrong,' she said, turning her face

away. 'And, just like usual, you can't accept you could be wrong about anything.'

'The only thing I was wrong about was thinking I could have enough of you. I want you, Jade. I want to make love to you. And I know that that's what you want too.'

'*I* want *you* to make love to me? I'd have to be some kind of mad woman to want someone who has accused me of all the things you charged me with. And you'd have to be some kind of loser to want to make love with someone you have such a low opinion of. What was it you called me—a fake? So fake I can't see straight—isn't that how you put it?

'And yet you now insist you want to make love to me. How does that work, when all you see is someone who's been put together by some crazy Frankenstein? Someone where you can't tell which bits are real and which are fake? How can you bear to even touch me now that you don't have to—now that your mission is completed?'

Dark emotion scudded like storm clouds across his eyes before he pulled himself back and suddenly released her. He surged away, his fingers tangled in knots behind his head.

'I had reason to think what I did. Even if some of my assumptions were misplaced.'

'What was that?' she asked, pushing herself away from the wall behind him.

'I said maybe I was hasty. Maybe I was too eager to colour you with Della-Bosca's brush.'

'I'm not sure I'm hearing this. You're not actually admitting you were wrong? You're not actually admitting that you misjudged me on yet another count?'

'Is it so hard to believe? The work you do, the way you look—how likely is it to be natural?'

She nodded. 'How likely, indeed?'

'I called you a fake,' he said. 'But I can admit when I'm wrong. I just didn't believe anyone who looked as good as you couldn't be one of your own clinic's best customers. I couldn't believe you wouldn't be living off a staple diet of surgery and Botox.'

She gave a short bitter laugh. 'Botox? Are you serious?'

And then it dawned on him. No wonder she looked so vital and alive! It was because, unlike just about every other woman in Hollywood, her facial muscles hadn't been rendered immobile by the injection of a paralysing agent. She was a natural beauty who didn't need anyone's help to look that way. And he'd judged her unfairly because of it.

He shook his head. 'What can I say? I just couldn't believe anyone as beautiful as you could have been born that way—especially working in your profession.'

'Well,' she said, adding a brittle laugh, 'if it makes you feel any better, I wasn't born this way.'

'What do you mean?'

'You once asked me to deny that I'd ever had a cosmetic procedure.'

'Jade, I—'

'The thing is, I didn't deny it.'

'You didn't have to. I was out of line.'

'No, I didn't have to. But that's not the reason I didn't answer.'

'What are you saying?'

She looked at him for a second. 'Wait,' she said,

before moving across the room to where her handbag lay on the benchtop. She pulled out her purse and flipped it open, tugging something out from one of the pockets.

'Look,' she said, holding it out towards him.

'Jade, I...'

'Take it.'

He took it and looked down. It was an old, battered photograph, worn at the edges. A photograph of a young girl, her face cast down, her eyes hiding from the camera. But there was a red mark on the photo, covering half her face, so the picture wasn't clear—he couldn't make out who it was.

And then he gave a hiss as it hit him.

The mark wasn't on the photograph.

The mark was on her skin.

'Who is this?' he asked. 'Why did you give this to me?'

'Don't you recognise her?' she asked. 'She's a girl people wrote off—because of the way she looked. Because of a birthmark that covered half her face people turned their heads away when she came down the street. People couldn't bear to look her in the eye, and when they did it was always with horror. Or, worse still, pity. Those people judged her because of the way she looked. She was worthless in their eyes.

'And you're no different to the people who shunned her because she didn't fit into their neat little view of the world. Because she's someone you summed up in a second simply because of the way she looked.'

He frowned down at the photograph. Her words burned in his psyche. It couldn't be possible—what was she trying to say? Nothing made sense. But there was something in the angle of the chin of the girl in the photograph, the slope of her cheek, something achingly familiar.

He looked from the photo to Jade and back again. 'Surely…?'

She laughed, and he knew she was laughing at him—and at his battle to come to terms with what was staring him in the face.

'It is me, Loukas. That's the real me as I had to live for sixteen years of my life. And that's the real me you apparently would rather see. That's the real me you would have preferred in your bed—someone unsullied by the evil hand of cosmetic surgery.'

He brushed aside her barbed comment—there was more at stake here than his own preconceived notions. 'What happened to you to give you this?'

She shrugged. 'Nothing "happened". I was simply born like that.'

'And there was nothing they could do then?'

'You have to understand it was a small country hospital and my mother was their main concern. She started haemorrhaging shortly after I was born. They tried to save her but just weren't equipped. By the time they transferred her to Sydney it was too late. They lost her *en route*. And my father was left without a wife and with a baby he couldn't bear to look at. He'd lost his childhood sweetheart and was lumbered with the ugliest creature he'd ever seen—something that could never replace the woman he'd lost, or ever stop reminding him of the pain.'

She paused for a couple of moments before continuing.

'And so for a while he refused to take me—and it looked like I would have to be adopted. But somehow someone managed to convince him to keep me, maybe because they couldn't find anyone else—God, it must have just about killed him.'

She stopped again then, as if thinking back. 'I think he really must have loved me to do that,' she said.

'What about when you were older?' he asked. 'They must have tried something in all that time.'

'Oh, yeah, they sure did.' Now her voice was more strident, almost bitter. 'Laser surgery was only new—experimental, really—and my doctors asked my father if I'd be game to give the new technology a try. I was only twelve years old, but I begged my father to let me do it. Because even if the people of the town had grown used to seeing me the way I was, had become accustomed to averting their eyes or masking their pity, still none of their sons asked me to school dances. Nobody wanted to be seen with me. And so I begged him to give me the chance to be as beautiful as my mother had been.'

He was silent for a moment. 'And it worked?'

She laughed, her face raised towards the high ceiling. 'No, it didn't work. Far from it.' She wandered out onto the deck, needing the fresh air and aware without looking that he was following her a few steps behind. 'I'm sure you know, but the way laser surgery works is to damage the underlying cell tissue in the skin just enough to encourage new cell growth. Ideally what will happen is that the cell tissue will be spurred into action so that basically the skin heals itself—'

He interrupted. 'But that didn't happen with you?'

'No. The technology was too new, too raw, and the technician misjudged the dosage. Instead of taking away the mark he used too high a dose. It burned my skin too deeply...' She trailed off, her blue eyes rippled with what he could tell was crushing pain. And still he could only imagine the disappointment of a young girl with a dream to be as beautiful as her mother. To be as beautiful as she could be.

As she should have been from the start.

As she was now.

'But there's no trace of anything. What happened?'

From his angle at the side of her he could see the grimace that screwed up her face, could almost feel the death-grip her hands had on the railing. He watched her take in a couple of breaths, almost as if she was forming her words. And then she spoke.

'I got lucky. There was a doctor visiting from the US who was said to be performing miracles with laser surgery, but the medical authorities at home were sceptical—nobody trusted the new technology after a series of bungled attempts. I wasn't the only experiment gone wrong, apparently.

'Anyway, somehow the doctor heard about my case, and decided I would be the perfect one to prove that laser surgery had improved and could perform miracles.'

'Weren't you scared to go through that again, after the first attempt?'

'I was petrified. I didn't want to do it. But that doctor explained everything so well—they were past the experimentation stage, they were really getting results—and convinced me that the surgery really could make a difference. I was sixteen years old with no family to protect me, and I wanted to go to university. I was a good student—my scar saw to that; there was no chance of boyfriends or distractions—and I knew I was good enough to get into medical school if I kept going. But I couldn't stand the thought of going like I was.'

She turned her face towards his. 'You see, I'd had enough of looking like a freak. I was growing up, and I wanted to be pretty. I wanted to have boyfriends and relationships. Is that so hard to understand?'

She wandered to the corner of the deck, placing her arms on the railing and looking out over the sand and surf, looking beyond the ocean, remembering her past and her pain.

He leaned against the frame of the open door, sensing that she wanted him to keep his distance right now. 'And this time?'

She straightened and turned suddenly, her eyes bright. 'It worked. It worked so well that no one could even tell I'd ever had a birthmark on my face. And I decided then and there that I was going to become a laser surgeon to perform miracles and change lives like that doctor had done for me.'

It was like a kick to the guts. So that was why she'd become a laser surgeon? *Not for the money.* He stood transfixed as another of his preconceived notions about Jade disintegrated into dust.

'So is that how the foundation came about? Was it your idea all along?'

She nodded, her face wistful. 'I knew how lucky I'd been. If it hadn't been for that visiting specialist I never would have had the chance to be treated by someone so talented, with the power to completely obliterate my birthmark. When I set about establishing the foundation, I wanted to make that possibility a reality for other kids who couldn't afford treatment and would otherwise be forced to spend their lives like I spent my early years—hiding my face—hiding from the staring eyes and the spiteful names. I knew how that felt. I knew exactly how much it meant to look normal.'

He nodded, the pain of her youth a tangible thing, weighing down her words. 'I see,' he said. 'I'm finally starting to understand why you ended up working where you did.'

'That's where you're wrong,' she replied, the wistful tone in her voice replaced with a sudden burst of bitterness, knocking him off balance yet again.

'You don't see at all. You won't understand anything until you realise that the doctor who performed that surgery, the doctor who made my life worth living and inspired me to do medicine in the first place, was none other than the woman you set out to destroy. My miracle doctor, the person I believed to be so wonderful she had to be an angel, was none other than Grace.'

'Della-Bosca!'

'The very same. It's ironic, isn't it?' she continued. 'I idolised her. I begged her to let me work with her. She was my own personal hero, and yet she turned out to be so bad, so corrupt. And I was too stupid to see it. I was too stupid to see any of it.'

Guilt twisted Loukas's gut and pulled down tight. What had he done to her? He hadn't merely misjudged her, he'd damned her from the start. And she was right. He hadn't understood a thing. It was like having blinkers suddenly removed—so much more about Jade made sense.

No wonder she'd been so intensely loyal.

No wonder she'd been so doggedly persistent in Della-Bosca's defence.

No wonder she'd fought tooth and nail against his every attempt to undermine her.

'Not stupid,' he said, pushing himself from the doorway and moving close enough to use the pad of his thumb to wipe a trace of dampness from her cheek. 'Never stupid. Fiercely loyal. Supremely protective. And now I understand why. Thank you for telling me.'

'But I was so wrong,' she remonstrated, her voice cracking, her face anguished. 'All the time I was defending her she was working to destroy herself. And I never saw it coming. All the time I was protecting her—oh, my God, Loukas, how many patients did I leave at risk because I refused to see what was happening? How many more could there been? Because I was blind to everything—she could do nothing wrong in my eyes—it was unthinkable.'

He cupped her face in his hands. 'Jade, don't.'

'And I never even saw it coming. If it hadn't been for you coming along when you did, how long would it have taken me to realise what was going on? And at what cost? How many more lives might she have destroyed?'

'Shh,' he soothed, collecting her in his arms, pulling her close against his chest. 'It's over.'

'How many more?' Her voice sounded as fragile and hollow as the sea urchins that sometimes washed up on the shore, their spines broken off, their insides empty, and their shells easily smashed, and he sensed instinctively that that was how Jade felt. And, as much as he wanted to, he knew he couldn't put all the blame down to Della-Bosca. He had more than his fair share to do with how she was feeling.

'She can't hurt anyone now.'

He held her like that, swaying gently in the morning sun against the backdrop of the constant flow of the tide, one hand stroking her back, the other caressing her neck, his fingers laced softly through her hair.

She'd fought against so much all her life, from such a tragic start, and against the odds she'd battled to make the most of herself. She was so brave, so fierce, so ready to defend those things she believed in—and she was suffering now because of it.

She was amazing. And he'd treated her as if she was a crook. He'd taken advantage of her and used her shamelessly in his quest to pull Della-Bosca down. But the hardest thing to take was that he had without question spoiled any chance he had at all to be with her.

So right now he would take what he could get. He could stay like this for ever, swaying gently in the sea breeze, holding a sun-kissed Jade in his arms. He wanted to lend her his strength, he wanted to see her fight again, he wanted to see her spirit.

And he wanted her for himself.

'Don't leave,' he said, almost before he'd acknowledged to himself that he wanted her to stay.

He felt her breath catch, her body still.

Without moving her head from his chest she asked, 'What did you say?'

'I said I don't want you to go. I want you to stay with me.'

She lifted her head and looked up at him, her blue eyes smoky and uncertain, searching his. 'I don't understand.'

He sucked in a breath. He wasn't sure he understood either. But he knew that whatever power drove him to want her couldn't be denied.

'You're right. I can't keep you here. But I'm asking you to stay with me.'

'What about your sister? What about all your concerns about me going to the press?'

'You won't sell your story. I know that.'

Her breath caught in disbelief. So finally he was giving her some credit for doing the right thing? But why now?

Her words came out in one breath. 'I didn't tell you all that just so you would feel sorry for me.'

'Who said anything about feeling sorry for you?'

Her heartbeat seemed to triple in an instant. If he didn't feel sorry for her then why else would he want her to stay? Here, nestled against Loukas's body, she could almost bring herself to imagine he cared for her—at least a little.

And that would be enough. After all that had happened between them there was nothing he could say that would make a difference to their future, but it would be enough just to know that he felt something for her. Just so she could take with her at least the thought that their nights together had meant something.

'Why else would you want me to stay?' she asked

tentatively, afraid of what he might say, afraid of what he wouldn't say.

But in the end it didn't really matter any more.

Because now it was all too late.

He rested his head on hers, his hands skimming her back. 'It seems I've got a lot to make up for,' he started. 'I was wrong about a lot of things. I was wrong about you.'

She blinked, straightening her back, forcing away the tightness in her throat. So this was all about paying his dues? He believed he owed her for misjudging her, and he thought he could set it to rights by being considerate to her and offering her a place to stay.

Nothing more.

She squeezed her eyes shut. But why should this latest revelation be such a surprise. Loukas had loved Zoë all along. His actions had made that beyond question. His motivations were now crystal-clear.

Because he still loved Zoë, had loved her even through those passionate nights Loukas and Jade had shared, Zoë had been the one driving his actions, Zoë had been the one he'd been missing. Only in seeking to avenge himself against Grace had he bothered with her.

And so be it. He didn't feel anything for her. At least they didn't have that unnecessary complication to contend with.

She'd learned her lesson already in that department. Because she'd imagined for a while that she loved Loukas, had even hoped that her feelings might be reciprocated, but that was before she'd found out that her being in his bed was nothing more than part of his plan to pull down Grace.

And just as he'd succeeded, and Grace's world had collapsed, so too had Jade's emotional landscape—shattering around her, scattering everything she knew, everything she held precious.

And now she didn't know what she felt any more. Now she didn't know who to trust.

She'd trusted Loukas for a time. And what had that got her? A few nights of pleasure and the bitter aftertaste of betrayal.

And through it all she'd trusted Grace. She'd set her on a pedestal so high, established her so far up on a scale no mere mortal could compete with, never realising that if anything went wrong it was a very, very long way down.

And things had gone desperately, irreversibly wrong. Now there was no way she could trust her own feelings. Now there was no one she could trust.

Not Grace.

Not Loukas.

And least of all herself.

She pushed herself out of the circle of his arms with a sigh and turned to gaze out over the bay one last time.

'I'm leaving,' she said.

CHAPTER TWELVE

IT HAD been a long day, Jade thought, as she turned her yellow Mini Cooper into the parking bay of her modest Balmain apartment. A tiring day, and yet immensely satisfying. Even after only three months in her new job, already she was making a difference to the tattoos that marred the arms, hands and even cheeks of her patients, slowly eradicating any evidence of ill-thought-out adolescent decision-making or the result of peer group pressure.

It would take many treatments and some time before the tattoo pigments were broken up by the laser into pieces tiny enough for the cells' own cleaning processes to deal with their removal. And it might take months or even longer for the tattoos to fade completely, depending on the size, colours and depth of the artwork.

But these guys had the time. They weren't going anywhere in a hurry. And by the time they were released they'd be rid of their home-made tattoos, the gang-inspired insignias, and any other visible artwork which would otherwise prejudice their chances of getting any job—let alone a good one.

She smiled to herself as she let herself into her apartment. Yeah, it had been a good day. She was doing work that was worthwhile. She was making a difference.

A Red Abyssinian cat bounded to the door as she

opened it, greeting her with a plaintive series of mews.

'Hello, Maxwell,' she said, reaching down to stroke the elegant animal's ears. 'How was your day?'

Maxwell wound himself around her ankles and complained some more about being left home alone without enough to eat before heading for the kitchen, obviously anticipating that Jade would take immediate steps to remedy the latter.

She laughed. 'Okay, Max, I know it's late. I'm coming.'

Once fed, the cat was quite happy to curl up quietly next to Jade on the small terrace outside. It was a warm night for spring, the air steamy, carrying the promise of a hot summer to come and filled with the sounds of live guitar music floating up from the nearby bar. Through the gap in the roof-lines she could see moonlight glistening on the dark waters of Sydney Harbour, until a late-night ferry cut a swath through the water, churning up the surface and chopping the reflection into shredded tinsel.

She breathed deeply and let it out on a sigh. It was a different life from the one she remembered in Beverly Hills. No more living in a mansion, no more Mercedes car, no more using her talents on the rich and famous, the celebrities and the already very beautiful.

And yet, for all the things she'd left behind, she was strangely content. She'd used only enough of her savings to buy this apartment and her car. She didn't need any more than that and, given the associations the money had with her former life, she didn't want it.

So she'd ploughed the rest into the programme she'd sold to the local prison authorities—and once she'd convinced them she was serious they'd matched her contribution dollar for dollar. Now they had the most sophisticated state-of-the art laser equipment and a constant line of hopeful kids wanting to have their tattoos removed, wanting a decent chance at life.

She was working harder and longer than she'd ever worked before, and for a stipend that barely kept Maxwell in cat food, but it was worth it. She didn't want for anything.

Except sometimes...

She snatched up her glass of wine and took a sip, flicking impatiently through the magazine she'd brought out, searching for anything that would grab her interest and dampen down her line of thought.

She didn't want to think about Loukas. Not now—not when she'd left that world behind, when she'd turned her back on him and walked away.

Because thinking about Loukas would get her nowhere. Wondering what might have happened if she'd agreed to stay was pointless.

So why didn't her dreams appreciate that? Why did scenes of Loukas's lovemaking keep playing over and over in her head, haunting her? Because it was so real in her dreams, so real... Only then she'd wake up to twisted sheets and the agony of knowing she'd been cheated again. Because it wasn't real.

It had never been real.

So why couldn't she simply forget him?

But the answer to that question was the cruellest blow of all. Because more than three months spent straightening out her head, trying to get a grip on her battered emotions, sorting out in her mind what was true and what was fake, what she wanted out of life and what she believed in, had only cemented in her mind one fact.

She loved him.

It made no sense. It made *bad* sense. She didn't even understand why. The knowledge was simply there, deep inside, like a flame that wouldn't go out— a flame that wouldn't be extinguished.

And the fact that it was wasted love, pointless, unnecessary and painful love, that taunted her in her weakest moments, that exploited her darkest hours, was no defence. It made no difference to how she felt. She loved him regardless.

'Damn him!' she said, picking up her magazine and wine glass. The cat raised his head and yawned, stretching out his front legs.

'Come on, Maxwell,' she said, holding the door open for him to follow her inside. 'Bedtime.'

'Dr Ferraro, you have a visitor.'

'Thanks, Cathy,' Jade said to the young administrative assistant, holding down the intercom button. She'd promised the prison board a report on the first few months' operations, and she'd been told someone would be sent to collect it. 'I'm just finishing up. Tell them I'll be right out.'

Jade completed typing up the last of the report and cleared her desk while it was printing out. She glanced down at her watch and grimaced. Maxwell would complain again, but it was Friday evening and they could spend plenty of quality time together this weekend.

She quickly scanned the report and signed it, before slipping the original into a large envelope. Her purse slung over her shoulder, she headed out.

'Sorry to keep you,' she tossed in the direction of the man looking down over the coffee table, his back to her. 'The report is ready...'

Her heart gave a lurch, the words dying on her tongue.

No!

It couldn't be.

Then he turned, and her world shook and changed direction. She blinked.

'Loukas?'

She realised she was still holding out the envelope, her arm suspended between them. Stiffly, mechanically, she forced it down to her side.

'What are you doing here?'

Something passed through his eyes, too brief for her to get a handle on, and his lips curved up into something approximating a smile. 'I came to find you.'

Cathy made a sound next to her, dragging her attention away from Loukas to the young woman alongside her. 'Um, is it okay if I leave now? Or would you like me to stay a bit longer?'

'Of course,' Jade said. 'You go. I'll be fine.'

Cathy looked at Loukas, her eyes narrowing a fraction in suspicion and curiosity, as if summing up this stranger with the sexy American accent, before looking back to Jade and nodding. 'If you're sure, then.' She took the envelope from Jade's death-like grip. 'I'll take care of this for you, too. Goodnight.'

The door closed behind the teenager and suddenly

it was too still, too close, the office suddenly too small now that Loukas's presence devoured the space. Only the sound of blood rushing in her ears, thumping through her veins, invaded the silence.

'How did you find me?' she asked.

She hadn't wanted to be found. Her body language, her nervous tension—she wasn't happy he was here. He buried a sudden kick of disappointment.

Maybe she hadn't had enough time.

Then again, maybe she'd had too much.

Or maybe he'd just got it wrong.

He seemed to make a habit of doing that where this woman was concerned. He hadn't expected to find her hiding out in a place like this, that was for sure. With its shabby redbrick exterior, shoved up against the boundary of Sydney Central Jail, it was the antithesis of everything the Della-Bosca Clinic had been. Tired vinyl chairs instead of Italianate leather sofas, flaking paintwork rather than original artwork, and barbed wire fences in place of palm trees.

And yet Jade herself looked vibrant, and so alive— despite her expression being guarded, wary.

'You weren't that hard to find.' Especially not when he'd been Googling her name almost every other day. Only for curiosity's sake, he'd told himself. Except since he'd discovered her new position in Sydney he'd been battling with himself to find a reason to stay away. Until he'd run out of excuses and the will to do that.

He glanced around the basic walls of the office. 'This place must be a bit of a come-down after Beverly Hills.'

Her chin kicked up a notch. 'Still judging everything by its appearance, I see.'

He nodded, unable to resist the urge to smile even while he was cursing himself for his mistake. But hell, he'd missed her arguing, and it was so good to see she hadn't changed that much.

'Touché,' he conceded. 'You're right. I hear you're doing good work here.'

Her head tilted to one side. 'I'm happy.'

He looked at her. Really looked at her this time. Beyond her overall look of well-being there were traces of shadow under her eyes, a hint of greyness marring the blue.

'Are you?' he said. 'Are you really happy?'

She drew in a ragged breath, her hands slapping against her trousers nervously.

'The police told me it would be months before Grace's prosecution went ahead. So what do you want?' she asked, her voice uneven. 'Why are you here?'

'We need to talk,' he said. 'Can I take you to dinner?'

She glanced down at her watch, running her top teeth over her bottom lip in a way that had him suddenly focusing on her lips, unsullied by make-up but for the slightest remnant of gloss.

It was a long time since he'd tasted their sweetness. It was a long time since he'd experienced their moist heat against his. He dragged in a breath. He was more than ready to experience those simple pleasures again.

'I'm sorry,' she said. 'I really have to get home. Maxwell is waiting for me. He'll get upset if I'm home too late.'

Something flickered in his jaw, and one eyebrow arched as his countenance turned darker.

He knew it!

He'd waited too long!

She'd found someone else to console herself with. Someone else to replace him. Someone else who would feel her legs wrapped tight around him, accepting him, bucking under him.

A bitter taste assailed him—the bitter taste of defeat snatched from the jaws of victory.

'You're living with someone?'

His bold accusation took her by surprise. Was that jealousy she saw in his face? Or simply inconvenience? The latter was much more likely. But how appealing a prospect anyway.

'You should have let me know you were coming. Did you think I could drop everything at such short notice?'

She could almost see him grinding his teeth together.

'Then *Maxwell* can come too,' he said. 'I'm sure we can find a table for three somewhere in Sydney.'

She smiled then, almost sorry for the aggravation she was causing him. *Almost.*

'There's no need. Maxwell will be perfectly happy so long as I get home and dish up his favourite food.' Her smile grew wider as Loukas's scowl deepened. 'Maxwell is a cat, Loukas. What on earth were you thinking?'

'How is your sister now?'

They were sitting out on her small terrace, Maxwell

curled up warily on one chair, surveying Loukas with a contemptuous eye.

The two of them had grabbed a bowl of pasta at the local trattoria and come back for coffee, both of them seemingly uncomfortable with discussing whatever it was that they needed to discuss in the company of others.

'She's well,' he said. 'Although Kurt didn't hang around for long once she made it clear she was staying at the house.'

'Oh,' she said, not entirely surprised. 'I'm sorry to hear that.'

He shrugged. 'It was hardly unexpected. The good news is that she's had time to talk to Con—Dad. He's finally realised that she's an adult, with her own life to lead. All this time she's been bucking against his control and going about it the wrong way, but now that he's acknowledged that she doesn't belong to him their relationship is really changing. I think they have a chance to work things out between them now.'

'And what about your father's run for the White House?'

'Didn't you know? He pulled out of the race.'

'He what?'

'I know. Nobody expected it. But he made the decision suddenly, a few weeks after Olympia came home. He's going to take a cruise next year with Stella—my stepmother. A long one.'

'You never told me what happened to your mother.'

'Didn't I?' He looked out over the view—at everything, at nothing. 'She died when I was four. A brain aneurism. I don't remember much of her.'

She shivered. 'I know how that feels.'

'I know,' he said, his eyes on hers, steady, compassionate. 'Anyhow, as a teenager I didn't take too well to having Stella around when my father remarried. And I know I always resented having a kid sister.'

'How's that going now? Is Pia talking to you yet?'

He smiled. 'Now that Kurt's out of the scene, more than she was before.'

'I still don't understand why you couldn't tell her why you were so opposed to cosmetic surgery. Didn't she know about Zoë?'

His lips tightened and added a question mark to his frown. 'She did and she didn't. She was barely fourteen when Zoë died. Naturally we tried to protect her from what was happening as much as we could. And when she got to the stage of wanting surgery for herself it was part of her alliance with Kurt and part of her rebellion against her family, because she knew how much we disapproved. But I don't think she ever appreciated why—until what almost happened to her.'

Jade dropped her eyes to the ground. If she'd thought Loukas's sister would be a safe topic of conversation, she'd all too quickly been proved wrong.

'I'm so sorry about what happened,' she offered. 'But I'm glad she's okay now.'

'I know,' he said. 'Olympia told me what you said.'

'What do you mean?'

'She told me that you tried to talk her out of having the surgery. She said that Della-Bosca overruled you and booked her in regardless.'

Jade nodded. So finally he believed her.

'Is that what you came all this way to tell me?'

'Partly,' he acknowledged.

'Only partly?' she whispered. 'There's something else you want to tell me?'

He pushed himself away from the balustrade and hunkered down in front of her. 'There is, as it happens,' he said, before collecting both of her hands together, cocooning them within his own.

'Jade,' he said, his voice low and rich, 'I need to know. Will you marry me?'

CHAPTER THIRTEEN

IT FELT good saying it. Better than good. He hadn't planned on blurting it out like that—in fact he hadn't been entirely sure what he was intending to say—but now that he'd uttered those four simple words it felt surprisingly right.

It was almost as if all the issues and problems he'd been wrestling with for months, jagging into his thoughts on the long flight over, had neatly sorted themselves out and filed themselves away. At last his mind seemed clear, his purpose defined.

'Marry me, Jade,' he repeated, more boldly this time, getting used to the feel of the words in his mouth and liking the way they tasted.

Her eyes were wide and almost luminescent, their clear blue light searching his own eyes. 'I…I'm not sure I understand.'

He shook his head and squeezed her hands. 'I know I have no right to ask, not after all I've put you through.'

'You're not the only one who was at fault. We both made some bad judgement calls. But I live in Sydney now, and I'm perfectly capable of looking after myself here. You don't need to feel responsible for me any more.'

'Is that what you think? That I'm trying to make up for what's happened?'

She took a deep breath and pulled her hands away,

pushing herself up from her chair and stepping around him. At the end of the small terrace she turned and gazed down at him, her hands clenched in front of her.

'Well, aren't you? You feel badly about what happened between us and you feel you should do something to compensate. But I'm not sure why you've decided marriage is the answer.'

Breath rushed out between his teeth and he twisted up to stand facing her. He held one hand palm up between them. 'I'm not doing this out of duty, Jade. I'm doing this because I want to be with you. I wanted you the first night I saw you and I've wanted you ever since. I haven't thought about anything in the last few months beyond how I could get you back.'

'You wanted *me*? I don't believe you. You wanted to avenge Zoë's death. You wanted to save your sister from the same fate and you wanted to pull Grace down. I never figured in the equation except as a conduit to achieving those goals.'

'Then believe it. That first night at the ball I did want you. I came to meet you, I admit, but I never had plans to make love to you until that night—until I'd seen you and I knew in an instant that I had to have you. I'm not proud of the way I handled it, or what I did, but I knew I wanted you so very much. And I knew that there was something between us even then. Because I saw the way you reacted. I *know* you felt it too.'

She frowned, her arms crossed over her chest. 'But you used me. You went to bed with me simply to get to Grace. You used me as a way to get to her.'

He rubbed his forehead with his hand. 'I know. That's what I had planned. I thought I could seduce my way into getting your co-operation, and expected to be able to walk away afterwards.'

'Which is exactly what you did.'

'No, I blew it completely. I thought that if I got close to you and seduced you you'd tell me everything I needed to know. But after three nights with you I was angrier than ever. I'd planned to sweet-talk the information out of you after we'd made love— when you were most accommodating, when you would least expect it—'

Her eyes flashed blue fire up at him. He felt her pain at his betrayal and her anger that he'd brought it all back.

'I told you I'm not proud of what I did. But I couldn't go through with it. Like I said, after three nights I couldn't bear the thought that you were like her, that you might be turning into another Della-Bosca.'

'But I wasn't!'

His eyes held hers. 'I know that now. But back then I was going crazy. I'd heard Olympia was back in the country, and word was she was about to have surgery. Which meant I'd run out of time with you.' He sighed and ran one hand through his hair. 'But I wasn't ready to give you up.'

'You mean you hadn't got the evidence you wanted.'

'No,' he said, shaking his head. 'That was what I convinced myself of, certainly. But what was more important was that I didn't want to lose you. I was angry with Olympia because she was coming back too soon, so that my time with you was limited.

'And I was angry with you,' he continued, 'because after spending time with you I wanted so much for you to be different from the person I feared you were. So instead of treading softly-softly, instead of taking things as slowly as I could with what time I had left, instead of gently eking out any details I could before you realised what I was about, I blew it. And then, of course, the more you defended Della-Bosca, the angrier I became.'

She thought back, her mind returning to that night he'd collected her after work and driven them to the beach house, his mood volatile, his eyes dark and hostile. And yet they'd enjoyed their most tender lovemaking yet. Only for the magic to descend into that sudden outburst—his demands to know what was going on with his sister, his seemingly mad accusations against Grace.

That night had signalled the end for them. He'd used her and deceived her and shredded her feelings in the process.

'It doesn't make sense. You were never going to have much time. And yet you had three nights, and you never once asked about Grace or the clinic. I had no idea what you had in mind. Why did you wait so long if you were so desperate to save your sister?'

'Because I couldn't bring myself to do it. I didn't want to risk making you suspicious. I wanted you just the way you were.'

She turned towards the harbour view and she laughed, low and bitter, into the balmy night air. 'You mean naïve, gullible, and easy to be taken for a fool.'

'No!' She heard him cross the terrace till he pulled up behind her. 'I mean warm, sensual, and every part a woman.'

She felt his breath stir the ends of her hair; she felt his words as low vibrations in her senses.

'I thought I'd found something special—*someone* special—and I wasn't prepared to lose you then. And the way you felt in my arms...' He rested one hand on her shoulder. 'I thought you felt something too.'

Warmth flooded her from where his hand rested, flowing through her flesh, his proximity triggering a tingling awareness in her skin. It was all she could do to fight the urge to be drawn against him.

She battled to hold herself stiff, trying to ignore the fact that with one small turn she would be in his arms, the one place she'd been dreaming about being for months. But she was sick of unhappy endings. Why would this time be any different just because Loukas had a guilty conscience?

'I thought I did,' she admitted, not wanting to give too much away, but wanting him to know something of what he had cost her—had cost them both.

'Then marry me,' he said, his hand squeezing gently, his fingers setting up a gentle massage. 'I'll make it up to you. I'll show you how sorry I am for causing you such pain.'

A chill iced her veins. With a quick twist she ducked away from his hand, putting distance between them on the terrace.

'No!'

'No?'

She pulled open the French doors and stepped from the terrace into the sitting room, unwilling to share this conversation with the entire neighbourhood and knowing without doubt that he would follow her inside. 'No, I won't marry you. Why is this offer any different to the offer you made before I left LA? You wanted me to stay then because you felt bad about what you'd done. *Because you felt bad.*

'And now you're here, hounding me to marry you, for heaven's sake, on the basis that you can show me how sorry you are. What do you think I am, Loukas, your responsibility of the week? Someone to make you feel better? To make you feel useful?'

'What the hell's that supposed to mean?'

'Come on. You know you have an over-active sense of responsibility—look how you protected your sister, and fought to seek justice for what had happened to Zoë. And now Pia is safe, and you've avenged Zoë, so you need another cause—you need another responsibility. You want to save me from my disappointment, save me from my hurt, and you think marrying me will be a convenient way to do that and absolve your guilt!

'Well, I don't want to be your next project, thank you very much. And I certainly don't want someone to feel like he should marry me to make up for the past.'

He stared at her across the room, his dark features shadowed in the low light. 'But that's not the reason I want to marry you.'

She blinked, waiting. 'It's not?'

He was shaking his head, moving closer. 'Although I can see why you might think that.'

'But you said you wanted to make it up to me.'

'And I do.' He stopped in front of her and reached

a hand out to cup her cheek, holding her face in his hand. 'I want to take years and years to make it up to you. I'm planning on making it up to you for a very long time.'

'But then...why?'

His eyes held hers and she saw something new there, something deep and wonderful and powerfully magnetic that drew her closer.

'Because I learned something after you'd gone.' A second hand joined the first and she felt his fingers caress her skin, spreading their tingling heat to every part of her. 'I recognised at last that all along, all the time I'd been thinking I was in charge, I had been falling further and further out of control.

'I acted crazily because I *was* crazy. I was angry with you because I wanted you, and knew you would never want me after what I'd done; I dragged you to the beach house in a pretence of protecting my sister's privacy because I couldn't bear to let you go, and I asked you to stay because I was afraid I'd never see you again.

'And it only occurred to me once you'd left why I was so desperate to keep you.'

She held her breath as she still waited, afraid to break the spell of his eyes on hers, afraid to break the magic sound of his words.

'I was mad with grief after you left. And I tried to forget you, telling myself that I'd get over you, that you hated me.' His eyes searched her face. 'You don't hate me, do you?'

Her lips stretched tight. 'Oh, I tried,' she admitted. 'I truly wanted to at times—but, no, I don't hate you.'

His features relaxed and he let his hands slip to her

shoulders, his fingers hypnotically stroking her nape. She watched his mouth, now so close, as she breathed in his scent, everything working together to intoxicate her senses.

'Good,' he said, 'because I couldn't get over you. And then finally I worked out why.' His hands slipped down her arms until he had each of her smooth hands in his own and he wove their fingers together.

'Because I fell in love with you. And I fell so hard I didn't even see what hit me. But I think I knew from the first moment we met that you were the one.' He pulled her closer so that they were almost touching, his lips to her cheek, her mouth against the seductive rasp of his chin.

'I love you, Jade, and I want to spend the rest of my life with you. I want you to be my wife.'

And then his lips dipped lower and his mouth sought hers, and she was lost in the heady feel of his kiss and the warm bloom of love that burst into life inside her.

She wanted to give herself up entirely to the feeling; she wanted to let herself go in the wonder of his announcement. But there were more questions to be answered, more ghosts to put to rest, and breathlessly she pulled away, her senses reeling, her bones close to fluid.

'I don't understand. I was so sure you still loved Zoë. I thought there was no room for anyone else.'

He pulled back a little, his eyes thoughtful, one hand playing in her hair, absently running the length between his fingers. 'I think I'll always love Zoë. She'll always be special. But I've done what I set out to do and that part of my life is closed now. Do you understand?'

'I think I do. I went out to Yarrabee a few weeks after I came back. I went and walked around the town. I went back to my old school and to the place we once lived. I sat at my parents' graves and I talked to them both for a while. I haven't done that for so long. And it helped me to understand that I could finally put all the disappointments and bitterness about the past away. I didn't have to change my accent and deny my origins. I didn't have to pretend to be someone else, to fit someone else's pattern. I decided I could just be me.'

She looked up at him. 'You made me see that, Loukas. It was you who made me realise that I should just be myself.'

He smiled. 'You know, I never thought I could love again. I never thought I would trust myself to it. But then you came into my life and showed me how good life could be, and I had to have more. I had no choice but to fall in love with you, even though it took me a long time to recognise it.'

He took both her hands again and held them between his as he searched her eyes. 'And the way you kiss me tells me that you must still feel something for me.'

She swallowed, nodding just enough to confirm that what he said was true.

'Then say you'll marry me? I don't care where we live—whether it's Sydney, LA, or any place in between. You're everything I want in a woman, Jade. You're everything I want in a wife.'

She pulled away, out of his grip, her nails biting

into the flesh of her arms. 'But you don't know that. You don't know that at all.'

'I know all I need to know about you to know that you're the one. I want you—exactly as you are.'

She squeezed her eyes shut and turned away. 'Please don't say that. Not yet, at least.'

'Look,' he said, 'I know it's hard for you. I know there's so much deception and betrayal in our history. But if I said to you that from now on there will be nothing but honesty, nothing but the truth, would that convince you?'

Her head dropped towards the floor, her hands linked over her brow.

'What is it?' he asked. 'What's wrong?'

She looked up, way up, casting her eyes beyond him into heaven, almost as if she was seeking some kind of divine intervention. And that was what she felt she needed right now. Anything to make this task easier. Anything to shortcut the pain and the shock, to head off the memories of Grace telling her that no one would ever want her as she was.

No one.

'If we're going to be completely honest,' she started, shoving Grace's words and her own doubts into the furthest regions of her mind. 'If we're going to deal with nothing but the truth, then before we go any further there's something you need to know...'

CHAPTER FOURTEEN

'I HAVEN'T been completely honest with you.'

Darkness swirled heavy and muggy in his thoughts, threatening to dampen and weigh down the exhilaration of knowing that he was close to his goal, that he was so very close to having her agree to become his wife.

And damned if he was getting this close only to lose her again!

'What do you mean?'

'I mean there's something I haven't told you yet that you should know before you even think about marrying me. Something that may change your mind completely.'

'How could anything you say now make a difference? Nothing could test us more than what we've already been through together.'

'Believe me,' she said with a hollow laugh, 'it's happened before. I know it can make a difference, and that it might make a difference to you.'

He moved closer, impatience giving his words an aggressive beat. 'Then get it over with. What is it that I should know?'

She hesitated a moment, her top teeth raking over her lip while she took a steadying breath. Then, 'Do you remember the photograph I showed you—the one taken before Grace had treated me?'

'I remember it. And I remember how I behaved,

because I assumed whatever procedures you'd had had been purely for cosmetic reasons. I was wrong. I told you that.'

She nodded, her face drawn tight. 'You did. But do you also remember I told you that the first attempt with laser surgery didn't work?'

'You said they misjudged the dosage.'

'That's right. Instead of renewing the skin, they damaged it beyond repair. Instead of removing the mark, they made it permanent.'

He shook his head. Surely that couldn't be right? 'But now it's gone—all trace of it!'

Her eyes turned apologetic. 'Well, you see, while the laser technicians were confident about the new technology, it was still basically experimental. But at least they had the sense to practise their new-found wizardry somewhere it couldn't be seen—just in case.'

His mind battled for reason. If she had a scar elsewhere he would have seen it. He'd made love to her plenty of times. He'd peeled her clothes from her. He'd seen her naked —

No, he hadn't!

Every time he'd tried to get her into the shower with him, or reached for the light, she'd slipped away on some pretext—under the sheets or into a robe. He'd felt her skin, he'd made love to every inch of her with his mouth, but he'd never actually *seen* her with her clothes off. Not in the light.

How could he not have realised?

She stood waiting before him, uncertainty and fear tainting her extraordinary features.

'Show me,' he said.

Someone's heart was hammering. His or hers? He couldn't be sure. She turned then, reaching her arm to the dimmer switch. His own hand stopped hers halfway there.

'No,' he told her. 'No more hiding.'

She hesitated, her eyes looking to the light, as if to plead that it was too bright in here, too exposed.

'Trust me,' he said, returning her hand to her side.

He saw her swallow, saw the shuddering movement in her throat and the tremulous acquiescence in her eyes. Her fingers fluttered to the hem of her shirt. They fumbled for the first button, struggling with the task, finally pushing it through.

Six times her fingers repeated the same jerky action, her eyes not leaving his. Six times he wished he could do more to help than merely stand there, waiting, feeling her anguish, feeling his own tension kick up with the quiet release of each button.

How bad could it be that she would hide herself away as she had done? How bad could it be that she would be so, so afraid?

He sucked in a breath and steeled himself for the truth.

Tears pricked at her eyes, but she wouldn't shed them—not now, not with him here. When he was gone there would be time enough for tears. She tried to will her hands to pull back her shirt, but her hands seemed stuck, somehow uncooperative.

And then his hands covered hers, squeezing them gently within his own. 'Let me,' he said.

Then, keeping his eyes locked on hers, he peeled back the sides of her shirt, scooping the fabric over her shoulders and down her arms, letting it fall to the floor behind her.

She squeezed her eyes shut against a fresh rush of tears and waited for the inevitable reaction. Scenes played through her head. She was back in Garry's car—her satin dress catching on the cracked vinyl seats, the smell of quick sex competing with spilt motor oil and last week's discarded hamburger wrapper—and then came his startled discovery and his cries of *freakgirl*, loud in her memory.

And then she heard something else, something happening right here and now—a hissed intake of breath. She stiffened, turning her face to the ceiling, her eyes still shut, preparing herself for the inevitable.

Preparing herself for the end.

But she was completely unprepared for his touch.

So feather-light and yet so powerful, the pads of his fingers traced over her skin, slowly following what she knew to be the dividing line between the scars and her unblemished skin. From one side to the other his fingers swept, following every curve, rounding every dip, setting her skin to tingling and compounding her fears.

Why would he be taking so long?

Because each second longer tortured her more as she waited for his certain rejection. Each second longer made her pain that much more acute.

And yet rejection didn't come. Instead his fingers continued their circuit up her ribcage, to where the line of the scar disappeared under the lace of her bra.

Suddenly she was aware that he'd dropped to his knees before her, and her eyes snapped open. She looked down to see his fingers deftly releasing the front clasp before gently, almost reverentially, he peeled the fabric away.

She held her breath as his hands skimmed up from her waist to capture a breast in each hand—one milky white, the other stained mottled red—his thumbs lazily stroking over the nipples, peaking them, rendering them firm. She swayed and reached for his shoulders—anything to anchor her against this tidal swell of feeling, this conflicting rush of emotion, of relief, of arousal.

Then he dropped his head, and she gasped when it was his mouth she felt on her nipples, his liquid tongue circling first one and then the other, giving them both equal time, equal attention, as if they were no different, as if they were the same.

And all the while his eyes remained open.

'You're beautiful,' he said, kissing the space between her breasts, setting her skin alight with the unrelenting pressure of his mouth and the intimate caress of his hot breath. 'All of you. Don't ever believe you're not.'

'You mean that?' she asked, her voice cracking as his mouth and hands continued their worshipful exploration. 'You really don't mind?'

He looked up at her then, studying her face before pushing himself to his feet and taking her face in his hands.

'I love you, Jade. How could this make a difference? I travelled halfway around the world to tell you I loved you and to see if you would let me back into your life. So how could something this insignificant change how I feel about you, when you are so much a part of me and I'm a part of you?'

And the tears that she'd been holding back, the tears that she'd promised herself she'd only shed alone, sprang forward to flood her eyes and spill down her cheeks. Only now they were tears of joy, tears of happiness, for what she'd found, for the man she'd found, and for the love she had for him—love that she now knew was reciprocated.

'What's the matter?' he asked as she pressed her head into his shoulder to hide her face. 'Have I said something wrong?'

She shook her head and peeled herself away from him, barely able to form the words but knowing she could finally tell him.

'No, you said everything totally right.' She looked up into his beautiful dark eyes, saw past their concern to the love shining down on her. 'I love you, Loukas.'

And his eyes lit up as if she'd gifted him the very best the world had to offer.

'You do?'

She smiled through the streaks of her tears. 'I do. Even though I tried to hate you, even though I told myself I couldn't trust my feelings, and to forget you, I couldn't do it. I love you so much, and right now, at this moment, I love you more than ever.'

'Then you'll marry me?'

'Just as soon as you want.'

'Oh,' he said, sweeping her up into his arms, 'I want…'

And then his lips found hers, and they sealed their commitment with a kiss that rocked her soul, leaving her breathless with even more discoveries.

Because how much more did a kiss mean when you loved someone and you'd discovered your love was returned? And how much more did a kiss mean when the past was gone and dealt with, and everything that lay ahead was brand-new and shiny, full of promise and expectation and hope?

And then his kiss deepened and her needs turned more immediate, more carnal. His hands traversed her back, crushing her breasts to his chest, travelling down to cup her close against his hardness.

Her heart swelled with wonder and the knowledge that his words of love weren't just words, but that he wanted her, in spite of her imperfections, just as much as she wanted him.

'I've missed you so much,' he said, his breath and his voice ragged and edgy. 'Make love with me, Jade. Make love with me tonight.'

'I want to,' she replied, thinking back to an earlier night that now seemed so very long ago before dropping her lashes to her cheek. 'But I'm not protected.'

He swung her up into his arms, the gleam in his eye telling her he remembered her coyness at that first meeting, and that this time too would be a first meeting of sorts—a first meeting of two souls who were destined for each other and who could finally acknowledge the inevitability of it.

'It's not a problem,' he said. 'I'm planning on being all the protection you'll ever need.'

'That's fine by me,' she said, as his lips drew closer once more. 'Because, like I told you, when I play, I play for keeps.'

His lips pressed warm and insistent upon hers, filling her with the essence of him and with his promise to cherish her for ever. Then he drew back just a fraction.

'And that's just the way I want it.'

HARLEQUIN®
Presents

The world's bestselling romance series...
The series that brings you your favorite authors,
month after month:

Helen Bianchin...Emma Darcy
Lynne Graham...Penny Jordan
Miranda Lee...Sandra Marton
Anne Mather...Carole Mortimer
Susan Napier...Michelle Reid

and many more uniquely talented authors!

Wealthy, powerful, gorgeous men...
Women who have feelings just like your own...
The stories you love, set in exotic, glamorous locations...

HARLEQUIN®
Presents

Seduction and Passion Guaranteed!

HPDIR104

Coming Next Month

HPCNM0606